Twelve Miles from Alice

Twelve Miles from Alice

Stephen J Anderson

Copyright

For Rachel, Thomas, George and Amelia

Preface

A TOP SECRET cable, sent from the Washington office of the Australian Security and Intelligence Organisation (ASIO), arrived at ASIO's headquarters in Melbourne on 8 November 1975. It read as follows:

"On 2 November the PM of Australia [Gough Whitlam] *made a statement at Alice Springs that the CIA had been funding Doug Anthony's National Country Party. On 4 November the U.S. Embassy in Australia categorically denied that CIA had given money.... On 6 November the Prime Minister publically repeated the allegation that CIA money had been used to influence domestic Australian politics. ...CIA cannot see how this dialogue can do other than blow the lid off those installations in Australia where the persons concerned have been working, particularly the installation at Alice Springs. ...The CIA feels grave concern as to where this type of public discussion may lead. The Director-General* [of ASIO] *should be assured that <u>CIA does not lightly adopt this attitude</u>."*
[The National Times, Nov. 8-14, 1985, underlining mine]

Seventy-two hours later the Queen's representative in Australia, Governor-General Sir John Kerr, dismissed Prime Minister Gough

Whitlam and replaced him with the Leader of the Opposition, Malcolm Fraser.

There have been many claims that the CIA, with support from Britain's MI6, orchestrated Whitlam's dismissal because he had threatened to close the American satellite tracking installation near Alice Springs, commonly known as Pine Gap. Such conspiracy theories have persisted for over forty years, and it is easy to see why. As WikiLeaks founder Julian Assange and former National Security Agency contractor Edward Snowden have revealed, CIA operations at Pine Gap allowed America to spy on virtually everyone.

In so far as Whitlam threatened to close Pine Gap, it was an off-the-cuff remark made to the American Ambassador following a heated exchange about America's conduct of the Vietnam War. Publicly, Whitlam stated he had no intention of closing Pine Gap—he simply wanted all information gathered at the base to be shared with the Australian government.

Would the CIA have waged a secret war against one of its closest allies to prevent the possible closure of Pine Gap? Could there be another reason why the CIA wanted to remove Whitlam, one far-reaching enough to secure the support of MI6? These questions are explored here in a story set against the background of Whitlam's dismissal. Elements of the story are based on real events but what follows is a work of fiction, with characters that are either invented or, if real, used fictitiously.

Part I

1. Martindale

Friday 27 June 1975, Canberra

The first light of day broke his dream with all the grace of a rabid dog. Waking in sweat. Alone. An empty whiskey bottle on the floor nearby. Without raising his head or even opening his eyes, George Martindale reached out and slapped the alarm clock, foiling its promised song. The first anniversary of his wife's death needed no cue. Martindale's only hope for the day was to see it end.

*

With less than four hours to go before Martindale's wish was granted, he faced the Prime Minister's closed door with his arm raised and hand moulded into a fist, ready to knock. But he didn't. His fist collapsed as the lobby's smell of polished wood hit his empty stomach and booze-sodden head. He shut his eyes with a groan and saw his wife floating face down in the waters of Lake Burley Griffin. He groaned once more, not from torment or sorrow but from anger—anger at the cost of keeping hidden the truth of her death.

'George?' came a gentle voice from behind.

Martindale turned.

The Prime Minister's private secretary, Mrs Henderson, was standing inside the main entrance to the lobby. A stout woman in her mid-fifties with permed grey hair, she resembled more a headmistress of an exclusive girls' school than a parliamentary aide. 'Did you want to see Mister Whitlam?' She spoke with a pronounced British accent.

His mind searched for a suitable excuse for standing by the Prime Minister's office, muttering to himself like a madman at a bus stop.

'He is free if you need to see him, George.'

'No, it doesn't matter. I'm meeting with him tomorrow morning, anyway.'

'Very well.'

'I didn't realise how late it was,' he added as glib justification for his odd behaviour.

'Yes, it is late. That young lady of yours must have the patience of Job to put up with the working hours you keep.'

He returned a grin tinged with alarm and said, 'I wish she did.'

'In that case, George, I wouldn't keep her waiting *too* much longer.' She gave her trademark smile, a smile that lifted her round cheeks but never quite reached her eyes.

His gaze drifted to one side, unfocussed.

'Is something the matter?' she asked.

'No . . . I was just wondering how you knew Kate was waiting for me.'

'Don't you remember our conversation this morning?'

'About what?'

'Katherine.' Her eyebrows drew together. 'You told me you were taking her to dinner and a nightclub.' She made an elaborate show of checking her watch. 'You had better get a move on, George.' With that, she turned and disappeared into her office, opposite the Prime Minister's.

Martindale tried to recall the conversation but couldn't remember seeing Mrs Henderson at all that morning. Not that he doubted her word—that morning's alcoholic fog had been particularly thick.

He faced Whitlam's door once more. No sooner had he done so, his shoulders withered like a punctured balloon. 'Oh, fuck it.' He walked out of the lobby, back to his office in the West Block of Parliament House.

*

Geoffrey Palmer, a twenty-four-year-old Fulbright Scholar from Piedmont, California, was sitting in Martindale's anteroom, clutching a dark leather folder as if it contained his life savings.

'Sorry, Geoff,' Martindale said, stepping into the room, 'I don't have time to meet now.'

'No problem, Professor,' Palmer replied, rising to his feet. His face was pale and decorated with a wisp of stubble, mostly confined to his chin and upper lip. His eyes were sea-green and full of life. 'I saw your light on and thought I'd wait to give you this.'

He handed the folder to Martindale. 'It's a draft of my thesis introduction.'

Martindale's eyes widened a notch at the folder's thick spine and delicately crimped leather covering. 'You don't need to bind draft copies, Geoff. A large clip would have been just fine.'

Palmer shrugged. 'My father's a bookbinder and he's always sending me these things. Keep it if you like.'

Martindale extended a half-smile. 'We could meet tomorrow for lunch, if you want.'

'Sure. In the dining room?'

'No, let's get out of this madhouse. How about we go across the road to the Promenade again. I fancy one of their burgers.'

'Sounds great.'

The phone rang from within the office.

'I must go,' Martindale said. With an upward flick of the folder, he added, 'I'll try to read some of this before we meet . . . say, one o'clock?'

'Perfect.'

'But do us a favour this time, Geoff.'

Palmer's head twisted a little.

With a grin that held both the mark of a father and the diligence of a teacher, Martindale said, 'Look to the right before crossing the road.'

'Oh, yeah . . . sorry about that.' Palmer's voice dwindled as his face reddened.

Martindale was heading for the phone when it stopped ringing. He grimaced and dialled a local number, but got an engaged tone. He gathered up some papers lying bare on his desk and, together with Palmer's thesis, bundled them into his briefcase and left.

With renewed pace he walked down the empty corridor of the West Block, past the Cabinet Room, across King's Hall and out of Parliament House.

Heavy rain bombarded Canberra. Martindale used his briefcase for cover while running down the steps and across the car park to his Toyota Corolla. 'Damn it,' he yelled, tugging at the keys snagged on the torn lining of his jacket. Late, knackered and now soaked through. 'Shit!'

2. Palmer

Palmer sat in his car at the far end of the parking lot, gazing through the rain-swept windscreen at the twisted contours of Parliament House. In the brief moment of clarity that followed each stroke of the wipers, he watched Martindale struggle into his car and drive away into the night. It was eight-thirty.

Turning his eyes to the Prime Minister's lit office, he gave a small shake of his head. What the hell was he about to do? After a solemn minute spent biting the inside of his cheek, his resolve set in. 'At least give me a break, Mister Whitlam, and go home.'

To deaden the wait and counter the relentless din of the rain, Palmer switched on the radio. The tune playing was immediately familiar, but it took a moment for him to register the song's lyrics: *You won't find another fool like me*. Taut lips gave way to an uncertain smile.

As the final bars of the song faded, Whitlam walked out of Parliament House—unhurried by the rain and head held high—and into a waiting Mercedes-Benz bearing the number plate C1. Seconds later, the Mercedes sped out of the car park and into the darkness of Langton Crescent.

It was eight-forty and a patrol would soon be completing a circuit of the House, including the Prime Minister's suite. Was there enough time? Palmer hit the off button on the radio with the flat of his hand and then checked the familiar contents of his overcoat pockets. His breath came fast and ragged. 'All right,' he said in a distant voice, the song's lyrics slicing through his head. He hopped out of the car and made a rain-drenched dash for the steps of Parliament House.

*

'Back so soon?' the grey-bearded guard said from behind his desk in King's Hall, a half-eaten sugar doughnut in his hand.

Palmer approached the guard with the wide-eyed stare of a lost child. 'I need a book from the library.'

'Working late on a Friday night, eh?

'I won't be long.'

'Take as long as you like, Mister Palmer. I'll be here all night.'

Palmer responded with a short wave, both a thank you and a goodbye, and walked through to the library.

He was in luck. The librarian was gone, there were no ministers or parliamentary aides in sight, and the door to the central courtyard was unlocked. Palmer snared a thickish book from the nearest shelf, then moved quickly through the courtyard and back into the House via the Senate Chamber. From there, it was an unchecked scamper to Martindale's office. He took a last look down the hallway. What if the patrol comes early? There was no one around, nor did any sound reach him. With a determined nod, he whispered, 'It's now or never.'

Palmer moved across to the locked inner office door and unclipped a large paper clip from his watchband. Unfolding both loops, he bent the wire in half, inserted one end into the lock and shifted the pins with the speed of a seasoned hand. With mild surprise at his own proficiency, he pulled down on the handle and the door opened.

Behind Martindale's desk, down on his knees, Palmer removed a hand drill, masking tape and a tube of glue from his left coat pocket, and a microphone and transmitter—together no bigger than a thumbtack—from his right pocket. He drilled a quarter-inch hole through the drywall, flush with the top of the skirting board, and stuck the microphone and transmitter into it. Using the drill shavings and glue, he made a paste in the palm of his hand and used it to plug the hole. He then mopped up the remaining shavings with the sticky side of the tape.

All materials rounded up, Palmer stood to survey his work. Someone would have to be on their hands and knees to notice anything unusual. He allowed himself a brief congratulatory smile.

'You found your book, then?' the guard said, his beard now decorated with sugar grains.

Palmer stopped in his tracks, his face a little sweaty. 'What?'

'Is that the book you wanted?'

'Oh . . . yes, thanks.' Palmer gave the book a little shake and walked on.

'Goodnight, Mister Palmer.'

3. Kate

Martindale's home was a two-bedroom apartment in a modern tower block at the foot of Black Mountain, a mile and a half north-west of Lake Burley Griffin. He called it home but, in truth, it was more of a place to shower and sleep.

He parked underground in bay '403', opposite Kate's bright red Mini Cooper in the visitors' bay, collected his mail and caught the elevator to the fourth floor. On entering the apartment, he kicked off his shoes, went through to the living room and tossed the mail onto a growing pile of unopened letters. A whiff of burnt toast tugged at his hunger. He grabbed an open packet of cheese crackers from the coffee table, stuffed two into his mouth and ate them while staring at a silver-framed photograph of his son, Timothy. Would Tim talk to him if he phoned? Will Tim *ever* talk to him?

A rumble of water from the *en suite* stopped his brooding. He looked at his watch and, with a modest sense of guilt, walked through to the master bedroom.

Kate's clothes were scattered over the unmade bed. *The Graham Kennedy Show* was playing on a silent television. He stopped in the doorway to the bathroom and leant against the frame. 'Hi,' he said in a sheepish voice.

Kate was lying in the bath trying to twist the hot tap off with her big toe. 'You're late!'

'Sorry.'

She pinched her nose and slid beneath the steaming water.

His eyes roamed over her willowy body until she surfaced, blowing the water from her lips.

She rubbed the water from her eyes and said, 'An important meeting with the Prime Minister, was it?'

'Almost,' he mumbled.

'What?'

'Nothing.'

'I've been sittin' in this icebox waiting for you, freezing my bloody tits off.' She squeezed some shampoo into her hand.

'Yeah, it is a bit cold in here.'

'A bit? I only got in the bath to keep warm.' She rubbed her hair and foam trickled down her olive-brown cheeks. 'Can't you afford heating?'

'The system was noisy, so I turned it off. Everyone's complaining.'

'No shit.' She caught him looking at her breasts and tilted her head to one side. 'You look like a drowned rat, by the way.'

Martindale moved to her. 'Is there room in there for two?'

Kate, rinsing the shampoo with cupped handfuls of water, shook her head. 'I need to get dressed for Julio's. Plus my skin's all wrinkly.'

'I don't care about your wrinkly skin.' He leant on the rim of the bath and ran his fingers across the back of her neck. She arched her body in response. Applying more pressure, he edged his hand down to the bottom of her spine, wetting his shirt cuff in the soapy water.

She twisted her head, her face now inches from his, and poked a finger into his dimpled chin. 'Towel please.'

He returned a crumpled mouth and said, 'I'll go and put the heating on, then.' After handing her a towel, he left.

'We've only got half an hour before it opens,' she called after him.

His image in the wall mirror beside the heating panel held him in check—an athletic body gone soft around the edges, dark brown hair singed at the side with specs of grey, tired blue eyes and a raised scar across his left cheek. He absently soothed the scar.

A burst of music from the bedroom jolted him back to the present. The nine o'clock news—Kate's news—was about to start.

Kate was standing naked by the bed, drying her hair with a towel and half-watching the TV. 'Hey, guess what?' she said as Martindale entered the room, 'I'm finally getting a new office away from the stinky men's toilet.'

'How did you manage that?'

'My sweet smile, of course.'

'It'd work for me.'

'No doubt, you dirty bugger.' She stopped rubbing her hair and held the towel against her chest. 'I reckon Howard only agreed because he doesn't want me to know how many times he pisses every day. He must have a bladder the size of a walnut . . . or a prostate as big as a watermelon.'

Martindale screwed up his nose in mock discomfort. 'What did you say earlier about something opening?'

'Julio's. You promised we'd go tonight to meet my friends, remember?'

'I haven't eaten yet,' he replied.

'Have some toast while I get dressed. That's all I've had.' Her eyes went back to the TV.

Martindale gave a low groan as he left the room. The last thing he wanted to do was spend an evening with a bunch of opinionated reporters in a noisy bar, but neither did he want to disappoint her. They had only met a few months earlier when, as a reporter for Channel Nine, she interviewed him on his role as Special Adviser to the Prime Minister. In reality he knew little about her, except that she was twenty-nine years old, enjoyed sleeping until noon on Sundays and telephoned her journalist mother in Perth every week. She also swore a lot, a trait at odds with her angelic face.

He collected his briefcase from the living room, walked into the kitchen and dumped Palmer's thesis on the table. Turning, he saw the empty bread wrapper lying on the sideboard. 'Thanks a bunch, Kate.'

On offer in the fridge was a jar of strawberry jam, two cans of Foster's lager, the remains of a takeaway carton of spaghetti bolognaise, and an unloved lettuce. He took a beer and drank most of it in one go.

The pantry contained half a packet of bran flakes and a can of peaches. He settled for the peaches.

Wearing flared black trousers, a pink blouse and a fresh towel around her head, Kate walked into the kitchen shaking an inhaler. She switched on the wall-mounted television. The news was still playing.

Martindale was leaning against the sink, struggling to encourage the last remaining peach onto his spoon. 'You look great, Katie.'

'Ta, thanks. I think the towel makes it.' She took two puffs on the inhaler.

A conspicuous name from the television grabbed their attention. Both looked up.

The Governor-General, Sir John Kerr, appeared drunk today at a reception for Shri Krishnamurti, the High Commissioner of India. Onlookers say that Sir John's speech was slurred and that he stumbled when trying to present . . .

'What a fuckin' galah,' Kate said. 'Why on earth do we have this guy?'

'He's the Queen's representative.'

'Yeah, but why do we need him?'

'Because we're part of the Commonwealth?'

'Smart-arse. Don't you think it's time we cut the apron strings?' With a glance to the TV, she said, 'We certainly don't need that pompous prick.'

Martindale shrugged. 'What difference would it make? Kerr opens a few public buildings and holds dinner parties for the great and good. Big deal.'

'Do you trust him?'

'Trust him?' Martindale replied with a screwed-up face.

Her eyes were etched with a curious glare.

'What's that look for?' he asked.

'Nothing, never mind.'

'Hmm . . . .' He took a breath. 'Do I need to get changed for this club?'

Kate scanned him from head to toe—grey suit, white shirt and tie. She frowned and said, 'You're almost dry now.'

'That bad, huh?'

'Nah, it'll do. By the way, I think you've got a crossed line. Freddie hung up before I put the phone down and I thought I could hear someone still on the line.'

Who the hell is Freddie? 'I haven't noticed anything, but—'

'Shh, hang on.' Her eyes fixed on the television.

There were fresh calls today for the Deputy Prime Minister, Doctor Jim Cairns, to resign his position for allegedly misleading Parliament. When questioned by Liberal opposition ministers, Doctor Cairns denied signing a letter that provided his friend and President of the Carlton Football Club, George Harris, a two and a half percent brokerage fee on any overseas loan he could secure for the government. Loans of up to four billion dollars were being sought. Sources close to the Leader of the Opposition, Malcolm Fraser, have confirmed the existence of the letter to Channel Nine News. Other sources have confirmed that the Prime Minister is now considering Doctor Cairns' position . . .

'What other sources?' Martindale asked.

'Cairns was set up.'

'What other sources, Kate?'

'How do you suppose Fraser got hold of that letter?'

'I have no idea. Could you answer my question?'

'No.' She looked back at the TV, now showing a commercial for Pedigree Chum dog biscuits.

Martindale reached up and hit the off button.

'Do you mind?' she said.

They were close now. He could smell her perfumed body. 'Parliament House leaks like a bloody sieve, Kate. Fraser could have got that letter from anyone.'

'The CIA gave it to him.'

'You wish.'

'They probably wrote it,' she added.

'I'm sure that would make a terrific story, Kate, and sell lots of papers. Just a pity it's not true . . . not that the truth matters much to reporters.'

'Oh, fuck you, George! What do you think we do? Sit around making up stories all day.'

'No, I—'

'You're a bloody shit, you are.'

'I didn't mean you. I meant—'

'Yes you did.'

'Katie, please, I'm sorry. It was a stupid thing to say.'

Her eyes locked on to the blank TV screen. She didn't reply.

'Jim's office is in chaos most of the time and he probably signed the letter without knowing it. That's what he's like. Anyway, why would the CIA give a monkey's about Cairns . . . or Australia for that matter? We're not exactly a superpower, are we?'

Kate looked him in the eye. 'You're so naive. How did you ever end up being a special adviser to Whitlam?'

Martindale blew a raspberry. 'Who knows? I never wanted the job in the first place and I still don't want it. As far as I'm concerned, getting back to academia can't come fast enough.'

'Oh, bullshit.' She paused before continuing. 'In case you've forgotten, Cairns led the protests against Vietnam. And he called Nixon and Kissinger murderers for bombing Hanoi.'

'I don't think it was quite that strong. Besides, Nixon's finished.'

'Kissinger isn't, and he thinks Cairns is some looney-tunes communist. The Americans don't trust him, George, and they definitely don't want him to succeed Whitlam.'

'So Kissinger got the CIA to forge some dodgy loans letter, then they all sat around waiting for Jim to say the wrong thing in Parliament, hoping the PM will sack him. Is that how it goes?'

'Yes.'

'Now who's being naive?'

'Not at all.'

'It's a little far-fetched, wouldn't you say? If they were that bothered, why didn't they just shoot him?'

'That was most likely their fall-back option.'

'You read too many novels, Kate.'

'I'm telling you, George, Cairns was set up. Maybe it wasn't the CIA, maybe it was. But one thing is for sure . . . he *was* set up.'

Eyes down, Martindale stroked the scar on his face.

'What?' Kate snapped.

'Nothing.'

'Yes, something. You always rub that scar when you're stressed.'

'I'm tired, that's all. It's been a long day.'

'Yeah, for me too, mate.'

'I'm sorry about what I said earlier, Kate, but can we please not talk about Cairns? I've been up to my eyeballs in that crap all day.'

'Oh, poor you.' She leant forward and gave him a cursory kiss on the cheek. 'We should go. I said we'd be at Julio's by ten.'

He put his hands around her waist.

She smoothed the lapel of his jacket with the flat of her hand, back and forth more times than needed.

'I'll shop next week,' he promised.

'It's not your clothes,' she said before clamping her mouth shut.

'Never mind me, Katie. What's up with you?'

'Not now. After our last barney, you'll think I'm completely crazy.'

'Probably,' he said with a snort. 'But tell me anyway.'

4. No voices

Palmer parked behind the foliage of a wattle tree in winter bloom, twenty yards beyond the concrete drive to Martindale's apartment building.

On the passenger's seat was a bulky, square-edged attaché case. He pushed on the central locking pin and opened it. Inside was a mass of switches, dials and cables, plus a reel-to-reel tape recorder. Plugged into the car's cigarette socket, the case came alive with soft-glow lights and a noise not unlike the hum of an overhead power line. He turned the volume dial halfway to maximum and flicked the receive switch. Straightaway, Martindale's voice rang loud and true.

For goodness sake, Kate, if something's wrong, tell me.

Very well, then. What do you know about Merino?

At the mention of 'Merino', Palmer's hand shot forward and pressed the record switch.

What are you talking about?

Above the further hum of the spinning tape reels, there was a faint sound of a phone ringing. Palmer leaned over the case, turning his ear towards its tiny speaker.

Sorry, that might be Tim phoning. I'll go and . . .

The voices stopped abruptly and, as the silence wore on, Palmer knew something had failed. He turned the volume up as far as it would go and closed his eyes to sharpen his ears for any voices. But none came.

5. Merino

Standing in the doorway to the kitchen, Martindale spied Kate holding Palmer's folder.

'Impressive binding for a thesis,' she commented, placing the folder back on the table. 'Was that Tim on the phone?'

'Wrong number. What were you saying before?'

'I was asking about Merino?'

He shook his head.

'Do you know what it is?' she asked.

'Yeah, a sheep.'

'Very funny.'

'You tell me, then,' he said.

'We think it might be the codename for a secret CIA base.'

'Who's we?'

'Never you mind,' Kate replied. 'Have you honestly not heard of it?'

'No I haven't. And my security clearance is the same as the Prime Minister's.'

'It exists, George.'

'Where are you getting this?'

'They've used it to target bombs on Cambodia, spy on the government and they—'

'Jesus, give me a break.'

She kept going. 'They've even planted a mole in Parliament.'

'Where are—'

'You're not involved, are you?'

His head went back a little. 'Why on earth would you ask that?'

'No reason, forget it.'

'Listen, Kate, if your editor is going to print a story like that, you'd better get solid proof.'

'You think I'm as mad as hatter, don't you?'

'No, but a story like that can—'

'Three days,' she said, 'and I'll have the proof I need.'

He took a lungful of air and expelled it. 'Show me first before you run with it, okay?'

Without meeting his stare, she returned a nod.

He moved closer. 'Katie . . . why don't we stay in tonight?'

'I knew this was coming. You don't want to meet my friends, do you?'

'I do, but not tonight.'

'You promised me,' she said with a mock pounding on his chest.

'I'll make it up to you.'

'How?'

'We could go sailing tomorrow.'

Martindale had not been sailing since his wife died, and his gesture was as much of a shock to him as it was for her.

She kissed him on the lips and said, 'Fair enough. But don't think you can dodge my friends forever.'

'Sure,' he replied.

'I'll go and get my stuff.'

'Don't forget your diary,' Martindale said. Fearing it lost, she had earlier in the week energised his apartment with ten minutes of flailing limbs and enthusiastic swearing, only to find it on the floor by the bed under a coiled mass of clothes.

'It's safe at work,' she said with a sheepish grin.

They came together at the front door and Kate held her face out to be kissed. He obliged with an easy smile and a hug. Then she was gone.

Martindale bolted the door behind her, turned and fixed his eyes on the telephone. He lifted the handset and dialled his son's number. It rang three times. His back stiffened and he shifted his weight from foot to foot. Another ring and the unwelcome greeting on the answering machine struck home. He stopped moving. 'Hi Tim. I was phoning to see how you are. Hope everything's all right. Call if you can. Bye.'

Keeping the handset snug against his ear, Martindale listened for several seconds. Could he hear anything? He set the phone down and walked back to the kitchen, scooping up his thick-rimmed glasses from the sideboard along the way.

Standing by the sink, he swapped his contacts for glasses and then poured himself a large Jack Daniels. He drank it in one swallow and poured another.

6. The Commander

'Go away, cat,' Palmer said as he keyed open the door to his studio apartment in downtown Canberra. 'Your master's upstairs.' The cat brushed against him, leaving a wad of hair on his trouser leg. He nudged it away with the side of his shoe, but with little effect. Placing a foot under the cat's belly, he gently lifted it away, hopped inside and secured the door with lock and chain. A single meow of protest filtered through. 'Sorry, little fella.'

The drab orange glow of the room's ceiling light heightened the food odors that greeted him. He set the attaché case on the floor, stepped across to the front window and opened it. The welcome burst of fresh air brought with it the fanfare of Canberra's Saturday-night boy-racers. He closed the window.

Palmer crossed the room—unloved, save for a few prints along one wall—and poured a glass of water from the kitchenette sink. Turning, his eyes travelled to one particular photograph and stayed on it while he downed the water. It was an uncomplicated image of a young woman with her back to the camera, standing alone in a barren landscape. Did it show blissful solitude or morbid isolation? He never could tell.

Below the photographs on a narrow side table sat a long lens camera, various colour filters, a cleaning cloth and a rotary-dial phone. He lifted the phone's handset and dialled an interstate number.

After two rings, a nondescript male voice answered, 'Identification, please.'

'This is Geoff Palmer. I have—'

'Identify yourself.'

Speaking slowly, he repeated, 'My name is—'

'State your section and handle.'

'Oh . . . section twelve, Cherry.' Palmer winced at his codename. Why couldn't it have been Maverick or Hawkeye, or anything other than Cherry?

'Is this a company phone?' the voice asked.

'Yes.'

'Go to scramble, please.'

Palmer pressed a button on the phone's bulky base unit. 'It's done.'

'Proceed.'

'I have intel that Merino might be compromised and was—'

'One moment, please.' The line fell silent for several seconds before the voice continued, 'I'm patching you through to the Commander.'

At the prospect of speaking with the section chief, Commander James Farnsworth, Palmer's shoulders snapped back.

'This is the Director?' boomed Farnsworth down the line.

Palmer's face crumpled at the roar hitting his eardrum. Playing by the rules, he shot back, 'This is Cherry.'

'What do you have on Merino?' Farnsworth asked.

'I managed to get a bug in Professor Martindale's apartment and—'

'We told you to tap his office.'

'Yes, I did. But I also planted a bug in the spine of my thesis, and he took it home with him.'

'Your thesis?'

'My cover, sir. I'm supposed to be his research student.'

There was no response.

'Commander?'

'What did you hear?'

'The professor's girlfriend was in his apartment. She's a reporter for the television News and—'

'I know who Martindale's fucking, now get on with it.'

With a doe-eyed stare of innocence, Palmer pressed on, 'She knows Merino exists and asked Martindale what he knew about it.'

'What did he say?'

Palmer grimaced. 'Um . . . .'

'Get on with it, man.'

'Something happened and I lost the connection.'

'Jesus H. Christ!'

Down the line, Palmer caught what sounded like an argument—at least, there was a lot of swearing. Was he about to get a lecture on the intricacies of installing bugs in books, or was he about to lose his job?

'You there, son?' Farnsworth asked.

'Yes.'

'Let's hope for your sake the bug in Martindale's office works longer than the one in your *thesis*.'

Although the words were threatening, the tone was benign and less deafening. 'Yes, sir,' Palmer replied.

'All right, we're done.'

'What about Miss Hamilton? I mean . . . she's a reporter and all. Isn't that going to be a problem for us?'

'You don't need to concern yourself with her. That's all taken care of.'

'Okay,' Palmer said, stretching out the word. What was taken care of?

'What are you doing tonight, son?'

'Pardon?'

'Are you going to any nightclubs or anything?'

'I wasn't planning to.'

'Good.'

'Why is that good?' Palmer asked.

'Let me know ASAP if the bug works in Martindale's office.'

The line went dead.

'And goodbye to you, too,' Palmer said as he plunged the handset into its cradle.

Standing by the phone, he cast his eyes back to the young woman in the photograph. Almost at once, the creases in his brow disappeared. Another moment later, his whole face softened with a smile.

A recurring sound at the front door broke whatever spell he was under. Palmer crossed the room and opened the door. The cat bounced in and leapt onto the nearest armchair, already covered in enough hair to make another cat.

Palmer sat on the edge of the chair and the cat immediately rolled onto its side. 'You know, little fella,' he said, stroking its head and back, 'Australia isn't as much fun as I thought it was going to be. Something's a bit rotten in paradise.'

7. Murky waters

The following morning

Martindale opened one eye as the morning sun trickled through a crack in the curtains and played across his face. Unsure of the strength of his hangover, he sat up slowly and squinted as he inched back the curtains. The sky was deep blue and the sway of a eucalyptus across the road signalled a crisp southerly wind, perfect for sailing.

His meeting with Whitlam was timed for half nine, and likely to last two hours. He could have a brief lunch with Palmer, leaving plenty of time to go sailing with Kate. Remembering his tactless remarks to her the previous night, he said aloud, 'You idiot, George.'

*

Martindale drove his Corolla along Commonwealth Avenue towards the bridge over Lake Burley Griffin, the traffic in both directions almost at a standstill. 'Not today,' he said with a slap to the steering wheel. His eyes darted between the dashboard clock and the road.

Dozens of onlookers were gathered on the footpath along the western edge of the bridge, peering over the railings at the water below. A throng of emergency vehicles lay across Barrine Drive and the wide grass verge surrounding the lake. A bright orange search and rescue boat sat in the water fifteen feet offshore. Alongside the boat, the choppy waters danced across the roof of a small red car.

Martindale glimpsed the tragedy with a quickening heart, though the chaos in his mind belonged to another time. He drove on to Parliament House, his face pale, his mouth dry.

*

Ministers, lobbyists and journalists were huddled in small groups across King's Hall. Martindale avoided all eye contact as he navigated his way through the crowd. He overheard only one topic of discussion: Dr Jim Cairns—whispers of the name hung like daggers in the air.

'Mister Martindale,' a recognizable voice called.

He dipped his head and walked on.

'Mister Martindale,' the voice called again, louder this time.

With the zeal of a dying sloth, Martindale walked over to Howard Rose, the Editor of Nine News and Kate's boss. Rose stood with four other men near the bronze statue of King George V: Lynch, Chipp and Killen from the Opposition Party, and Professor Julian Miles from the Australian National University. All were smoking. All had rigid smiles.

'Hello, Howard,' Martindale said.

Each man nodded to him, apart from Miles, who upturned his florid nose and grunted like an underfed pig.

'Troubled times, Professor,' Rose said.

'Nothing new, then.'

Rose discarded his smile. 'Has the Prime Minister spoken to you about his plans for Doctor Cairns?'

'Not yet.'

Miles grunted again. 'You must have some idea what's going on.'

Martindale shrugged.

Rose peered around the circle, his lips pursed and eyebrows raised, inviting comment from someone else. When no one took the bait, he said, 'Lying to the House is a pretty serious offence and I would—'

'Is that what happened?' Martindale interrupted. 'Doctor Cairns made it quite clear he has no knowledge of this so-called loans letter.'

Rose kept his eyes on Martindale, but didn't reply.

'Of course,' Miles said, grinning, 'that's not the only problem Doctor Cairns has at the moment, is it?'

Martindale remained po-faced while everyone else tittered like schoolboys passing around a copy of *Playboy*.

'You must know about his personal assistant, Junie Morosi,' continued Miles. He slid his eyes around to the others. 'I feel sorry for his wife, poor woman.'

'Yes, I'm sure you do, Julian,' Martindale replied. 'By the way, how's that lovely PhD student of yours? Clare, is it?'

Miles stiffened. 'She submitted her thesis several weeks ago, thank you.'

'No doubt, she'll pass with flying colours.' He made a show of checking his watch. 'I must go, I'm afraid.'

'Good of you to stop by, Professor,' Rose said.

Martindale twisted his lips into a smile of sorts, then promptly walked away.

8. No escape

As Martindale passed into the Prime Minister's lobby, the rumble of talking heads and false laughter from King's Hall gave way to an eerie silence. Something felt wrong.

Mrs Henderson appeared from her office and said, 'Go straight in, George, the PM's waiting for you.'

'But the meeting's not for another ten minutes.'

'He wants a word with you in private about Doctor Cairns.'

'Oh . . . .' Martindale felt his body stiffen. 'I wanted to get the exit poll results for today's by-election.'

'I'll do that for you. He said to go in as soon as you arrive.'

'Is it that bad?'

'Probably.'

Martindale turned and moved over to the Prime Minister's door. Before knocking, he turned back. 'Is Jim still coming to the meeting?'

'Yes.'

'Should be a lively morning, then.'

'Aren't they always?' she replied.

*

Jim Cairns arrived looking dishevelled in a crinkled beige outfit and lopsided tie. Bill Hayden, the Treasurer, arrived next in a tailored blue suit and clutching an inch thick pile of documents. Donald Maclean, the Minister for Health, and Fred Bailey, the Minister for Education, followed soon after. Mrs Henderson kept them waiting in the lobby.

Bailey poked his head around Mrs Henderson's door. 'Can't we go in yet?' he asked, tapping on his wristwatch.

'The Prime Minister is speaking privately with Professor Martindale.'

'It's after half past.'

'Yes, Mr Bailey. I am sure they will not be too much longer. Would you like some tea or coffee while you're waiting?'

'No . . . thank you.'

'Be patient, Fred,' Hayden said, thumbing through his papers.

Bailey faced Hayden. 'Be patient, my arse. What is it with this so-called professor? If you ask me, he's been a complete waste of space since his wife died. And *that* was a funny old affair and all.'

'Well, Fred,' Cairns said, 'no one's asking you, mate. So shut up and sit down.'

*

'I'll have the bugger's balls on a plate for this,' Whitlam said to Martindale as he passed Dr Cairns' letter across the desk.

Martindale read it without expression.

For the Attention of: Mr George Harris
... The Australian Government is interested in exploring available loan funds from overseas. In the event of a successful negotiation, which may

```
be introduced or arranged by you, we would be
prepared to pay a once only brokerage fee of 2.5%
deducted at the source to you...
```

'Well?' Whitlam asked in his familiar breathy growl, sitting forward.

'The signature looks genuine,' Martindale offered.

'A four billion dollar loan, for Christ's sake.' Whitlam's hands were poised ready to strangle someone. 'And that silly bugger promised his mate twenty-five *million* dollars.' The Prime Minister shook his head. 'I think Miss Morosi must have softened his brain, no matter what she may have hardened.'

'How did the Opposition get hold of it?'

'I don't know. You can't fart in this place without them knowing.' Whitlam leant back. 'Guess who phoned me last night?' Without waiting for a response, he continued, 'Stan Wirral from *The Herald*, warning me he's going to publish Jim's letter in the Sunday papers. And to prove Jim lied, he's publishing the Hansard transcripts as well.' The chair creaked as Whitlam held out his hand for the letter.

Martindale looked at the signature one last time before handing it back.

The Prime Minister folded the letter and slipped it inside his coat. 'Fraser has stuck the knife in well and true this time, and that bastard will twist it for all it's worth.'

'There are rumours the letter is a fake.'

'If only that was true, George.'

'I can't imagine Jim would lie, though.'

'He either lied or he forgot,' Whitlam replied. 'The silly bugger hates correspondence and signs everything as fast as he can.'

'Yes . . . I know.'

'Ah, sod it,' said Whitlam. 'We better let them in. I'll talk to Jim after the meeting.' He stood and walked around the desk.

Martindale stood and faced the Prime Minister. 'Jim's still coming, then?'

'If we're going to discuss the budget, we need to hear what he has to say. I'll sack him next week.'

Martindale lent back on his heels.

'Don't worry, George.' Whitlam gave two taps to Martindale's upper arm. 'Jim will survive. Not as Deputy PM, but he will survive. And so will that beautiful assistant of his.'

'Sure.'

'Which reminds me,' Whitlam said, 'how's Kate?'

'Fine, thanks.'

'You know, she interviewed me once about Australia's energy resources. Quite the tiger, eh?'

'Yes, she can be.'

Whitlam gave a chuckle and said, 'Come on, let's have them in and get the circus going.' He led Martindale to an informal seating area—two sofas and two armchairs around a knee-height table dressed with a plate of fresh lamingtons, side plates and napkins. 'Best snap up one of those cakes before Jim moves in for the kill.'

Hayden was first through the door. 'Good morning, Gough.'

'Morning, Bill. Come in, everyone. Help yourselves to a lamington if you're hungry.'

'Great,' Cairns said. He made a beeline for an empty space next to Martindale on the far sofa and grabbed a cake. 'Are these from June?'

'Yes, Jim,' Whitlam said, perching himself on one armchair. 'Best get in quick, eh?' The Prime Minister took a lamington and stuffed a goodly portion of it into his mouth, leaving a trail of desiccated coconut from the table to his lips. Except for Hayden, the others did the same. No one bothered with a side plate or napkin.

'I'll make a start, shall I?' Hayden said with a firm voice. He sat in the armchair opposite Whitlam, head high and with a pencil-straight back. He appeared confident, like a schoolmaster about to give a lecture on his favourite topic. Only Martindale, sitting nearest, noticed the small beads of sweat on Hayden's upper lip.

'Yeah, why not,' Bailey said. 'Let's hear the gloom first.'

Maclean chuckled.

Cairns, busy picking pieces of coconut off his tie, didn't react.

'Go on, Bill,' Whitlam said, eyeing another cake.

'Well,' Hayden said with an even straighter back, 'it should hardly come as a surprise that the economy is getting out of hand. Unless we take drastic action now, a substantial number of enterprises in the corporate sector may fail and the recession will deepen. As things stand, we're looking at a budget deficit of around five thousand million.'

'Whoa!' Maclean said. 'Are you sure about that, Bill? My department's expecting a figure closer to four thousand.'

'Well,' Hayden replied, 'my department can add.'

'Yeah, right,' Bailey said. 'And how long have you been treasurer?'

'Long enough, mate!' The beads of sweat on Hayden's upper lip were now visible to all. 'Look, Fred, I'm not—'

'All right you two,' Whitlam said.

'Jim?' Hayden said, looking across to Cairns for support. But Cairns stayed stony-faced silent with his arms folded and anchored to his chest.

'I trust,' Bailey said, 'you're not planning on taxing the buggers to death, because—'

'Quiet, Fred,' Whitlam said, 'and let Bill finish.' He faced Hayden. 'Give us the bottom line, Bill.'

'I'm not suggesting any new tax rises, Fred. But to achieve that, every department will need to cut spending by at least ten percent.'

'You're off your rocker,' Bailey cried.

'How on God's earth is that going to be possible in education or health?' Maclean asked.

Cairns opened his mouth to speak when there was a knock on the door. Mrs Henderson came into the room carrying a tray of coffee, with a blue plastic wallet tucked under her left arm.

'Ahh, June,' Whitlam said. 'You're just in time to stop this lot from tearing their throats out.'

She smiled but didn't comment as she put the tray down and gave the wallet to Martindale.

'Thanks, June,' Martindale said. He opened the wallet and removed the teletype printout within it.

'Great lamingtons, June,' Cairns said. 'Delicious, as always.'

'You're welcome, Doctor Cairns.' She glanced at the sole remaining cake and left.

'What is it, George?' Whitlam asked. 'You look troubled.'

'This is Reiter's first exit poll for the by-election in Bass. And it isn't good.'

'Bass has been a safe Labor seat for sixty years,' said Bailey. 'We don't have any worries there.'

'You think?' Martindale countered, holding the printout forward. 'This suggests a swing against us of around eight percent. If that's the case, we can kiss Bass goodbye.'

'George is right,' Hayden offered. 'We only need a swing of five percent to lose the seat.'

'You're so predictable, Bill,' Bailey said.

'The outcome of this election certainly is,' Hayden replied.

Bailey shook his head. 'I'm not wasting my time—'

'Will you two give it a rest?' Whitlam said.

An edgy silence filled the room until Maclean chipped in with, 'It'll be tight, for sure, but with a fair wind I reckon we should still win it.'

Cairns was pouring himself a coffee when he stopped, slapped the pot down on the table and said, 'Jesus Christ, they're not all bloody morons in Tasmania! They'll vote with their pockets, just like the rest of us.'

'The economy's not our fault, Jim,' Bailey said. 'The whole world's heading for recession. They can't blame us.'

'Yes they can, and they bloody well will.'

'Thank you, Jim,' Whitlam said. 'Clear and to the point, as always.' His hand inched towards the remaining lamington. 'Would anyone mind?' No one spoke and he scooped up the cake. 'Yes, Jim, the economy will hurt us. Of course, events over the past two weeks haven't helped matters.'

Cairns stared into his lap.

Two loud knocks on the door in rapid succession turned everyone's head. The door opened and Mrs Henderson cut in and made a beeline to the Prime Minister. She shot a glance at Martindale before stooping to whisper in Whitlam's ear.

'If we do lose Bass, Martindale said, with one eye on Mrs Henderson, 'our position in . . . the Senate . . . .' Martindale stopped as the Prime Minister, open-mouthed, looked directly at him.

*

That evening Martindale sat alone in his apartment, whisky in hand, watching a detailed account of the accident on the television. He thought back to the pain and guilt of his wife's death. He thought too of Timothy and his pain, his torment and their lost relationship.

Martindale gripped the crystal tumbler with such force that it shattered, slicing the inside of his thumb as it fell to the floor. He buried his face into the open palms of his hands. Two lines of blood and a tear trickled down the right side of his face, merging at the corner of his lips.

He shut his eyes to the news but could not escape the truth: Kate was dead.

9. The Coroner

The following week, Tuesday 8 July

The young girl's long brown hair floated behind her as she raced up and down the veranda of the brilliant-white house at the crest of the hill. With arms outstretched, she flew around the old rocking chair, once, twice, three times. Stopping, she peered over the iron railing at the lake below. Her eyes were wide with wonder as she watched the black swans dance across the water, gathering at the shore, encircling the unsuspecting tourists. She laughed aloud as the hungry birds snatched at the offerings of stale bread, nipping at fingers and bread with equal abandon. Then, without warning, she scooped up her dolls and ran to the bright red door that led inside. It wouldn't open. She screamed for help. No one heard her.

'Kate,' Martindale called, tossing in his bed. 'Kate,' he called again as the last images from his dream faded away. A moment later, the certainty of morning struck. He sat up. Drops of sweat covered his chest and he gripped a corner of the sheet to smother them. The accident report replayed in his mind.

Katherine Hamilton, winner of last year's Walkley Award for investigative journalism, and Frederick Saunders, a reporter for

Channel Nine News, were killed in a tragic road accident. Returning home after spending the evening in a local nightclub, Miss Hamilton apparently lost control of the vehicle and skidded off the road into Lake Burley Griffin. There are unconfirmed reports she may have been under the influence of alcohol.

Martindale shrugged off the blankets and, wavering like a willow in a high wind, walked to the bathroom. Steadying himself against the sink, he spied the bags under his eyes and the grey patches in his week-old beard. He groaned as if in pain, sidled across to the toilet and sat down to pee.

Twenty minutes later, showered and shaved, he completed his contact lens ritual, collected the unopened mail from the living room and left for Parliament House. It was five past nine.

*

Seated at his desk, Martindale scanned the Prime Minister's schedule for the day. Only an appointment with Rupert Murdoch stood out as unusual. Why was Murdoch here? He opened his briefcase and removed the mail and long-forgotten draft of Geoffrey Palmer's thesis.

He flipped through the mail, stopping at a letter from his university. Turning the envelope over to open it, his mouth dropped and he gave a double take at Kate's unmistakable scribble—wavy lines akin to birds in flight scattered about a child-like sketch of a sheep. 'Merino?' he said softly. The letters N and H filled the sheep's stomach. Someone's initials? He sank into the chair and closed his eyes. In the muted light, he could see Kate's red Mini floating in the lake. He opened his eyes to extinguish the image, but it wouldn't leave him. Nor would the TV reporter's words that Kate may have been drunk.

He sat forward and pressed the intercom for Mrs Henderson.

'George, I didn't realise you were in,' she answered. 'How are you?'

'I'm fine.'

'Are you sure? If there is anything I can do to help, you only have to ask.'

'I'm fine, June. But I need to see the PM?'

'He's with the American Ambassador at the moment, but I'll let him know you are here as soon as I can. Was there anything else?'

'Yes,' Martindale answered. 'Could you get me the coroner's office on the line?'

'Was there anyone in particular you wanted to speak with?'

'The coroner.'

'I'll put the call through right away.'

A few minutes later, a red light flashed on the intercom.

Martindale pressed the speaker button.

'Carl Schröder here.'

'Good morning Doctor Schröder. My name is George Martindale.'

'Yes, your secretary said. I assume you are calling about Miss Hamilton.'

'She told you that?'

'She didn't need too, Professor. I read the papers.'

Martindale frowned. Did everybody know his personal affairs?

'How can I help you?' Schröder asked.

'I was hoping you could give me more detail about Miss Hamilton's accident.'

A tapping noise emerged from the speaker, accompanied by some mumbled words.

'Is something the matter?' Martindale asked.

'The official report hasn't been released yet.'

'All I'm trying to do, Doctor Schröder, is find out whether Kate suffered or not.'

Other than a faint sigh, there was no reply.

'I'd appreciate anything you could tell me,' Martindale added.

'Yes, yes,' Schröder replied. 'One moment, please.'

Martindale caught the sound of a filing cabinet drawer opening and closing. He absently took hold of a staple gun from the desk.

'Mister Martindale?'

'Yes.'

'You understand that you are not to discuss this with anyone until the information is released?'

'Of course.'

'Good.' There was a pause before the coroner said, 'It is quite an interesting case, in fact.'

Martindale winced at the suggestion Kate's death was interesting.

'Alcohol didn't cause Miss Hamilton to crash, as such,' Schröder continued. 'Her death was the cause of the accident, not the other way round.'

'What?' Martindale squeezed the stapler, ejecting a tack onto the bright yellow notepad before him. 'I don't understand.'

'The only contusion on her body was across the right shoulder, but this was from the seat belt. Plus, there was no water in her lungs.'

'So . . . what are you saying?'

'I am saying Miss Hamilton was dead before the car went into the lake.'

Martindale's face twisted with confusion.

'Not so, her companion,' Schröder announced. 'His lungs were full of water.'

'But you don't know how Kate died?'

'Of course we do.'

Then fucking tell me, Martindale thought, sweeping the spent staple off the desk with the back of his hand.

'A full toxicology screening didn't show up anything except a moderate amount of blood alcohol.'

'I thought you said alcohol wasn't involved.'

'That is not what I said.'

In as calm a voice as he could muster, Martindale asked, 'How did Kate die?'

'I assumed you knew she was alcohol intolerant.'

'Which means what, exactly?'

'Miss Hamilton had a severe deficiency of Aldehyde Dehydrogenase, the enzyme needed to metabolise alcohol. Without it, even a modest drink can be dangerous.'

'How?' Martindale picked up a pen.

'She had a heart attack while driving the car. That is the most likely reason why she crashed.'

Martindale's pen hovered above the notepad, but he didn't write anything. What he was hearing seemed impossible to believe. 'She was only twenty-nine.'

'Yes, plenty old enough to be aware of her condition. We asked for her medical records, but they appear to be missing. Still, she must have known. Perhaps she was simply careless on the night.'

An image of Kate swilling mineral water loomed before him. 'She knew,' Martindale whispered.

'Sorry, what?'

'Nothing,' he replied.

'At the mother's request,' Schröder explained, 'the body has been flown back to Perth for burial on Thursday.'

'This Thursday?'

'Yes.'

'Do you have her address?'

'Don't you have it?'

'No.'

'One moment.'

Martindale waited, pen in hand.

'Missus Margaret Donohue, Lakeview, Wembley.'

'Lakeview . . . is that it?' Martindale asked.

'That is all the information we have.'

'Phone number?'

'Sorry,' Schröder replied. 'I can give you the address for the funeral if you want.'

'Please.'

'Saint Michael's Chapel, 50 Ruislip Street, Leederville.'

Martindale scribbled the address down. 'Thank you for your time, Doctor Schröder.'

Chin down, Martindale cradled his forehead with the fingertips of both hands. 'Careless, my arse,' he spat.

Mrs Henderson, standing in the doorway, gave a polite cough.

He looked up.

She smiled and took two steps forward. 'I just popped in to say the PM's free to see you now.'

'Thanks.' He paused a moment. 'Could you book me on a flight to Perth? I need to be there this Thursday.'

Mrs Henderson pulled a surprised face. 'My goodness, George, you really have been locked away.'

'Sorry?'

'The baggage handlers are going on strike tonight. There won't be any commercial flights until the weekend.'

He grunted.

'You may be in luck, though. I know Mister Murdoch is travelling to Perth tomorrow by private plane. I'm sure he wouldn't mind giving you a lift.'

'I thought he changed sides to the Opposition.'

'That may be so, but he's probably your only chance of getting to Perth by Thursday.'

'Hmm . . . could you ask for me?'

'Of course.'

'Thanks, June.'

10. Lies and promises

Prime Minister Whitlam extended his sympathies to Martindale, welcomed him back to work and agreed his visit to Perth. Then it was on to business. 'You know, of course, that Fraser's threatening to block our money bills?'

'I doubt he has the guts to go through with it, Gough . . . not without the general public behind him.'

'With Murdoch's press attacking us every day, it won't be long before the public flock to Fraser like rats to a corpse.' Whitlam's chest swelled with bravado. 'But I'll be damned if I am going to give in to either one of them.'

'You met with Murdoch this morning?'

'Yes. If you can believe it, he wants the High Commissioner post to London.' Whitlam added, with singular clarity, 'Over my dead body.'

Holding a lopsided smile, Martindale said, 'I might be traveling to Perth with him tomorrow.'

Whitlam's head nudged back.

'With the airline strike on,' Martindale continued, 'Murdoch's plane might be the only one flying.'

'Oh, yes.' Pausing, Whitlam added, 'I wouldn't sit too near the exit, if I were you.'

'No,' Martindale said with a chuckle, 'I won't.'

Whitlam leant forward in his chair with one elbow on the desk and his head skewed as though he was about to give away a state secret. 'If Fraser blocks our supply, we won't be able to govern for more than a month.' He leaned in closer still. 'We need to secure a sizeable loan or we're finished.'

'Rex Connor is a good man, Gough, but he's not up to the job of raising funds.'

With a vexed look, Whitlam replied, 'I've withdrawn Rex's authority to raise funds and have no intention of reinstating it. In any event, I don't consider this mess to be Rex's fault. His only error was trusting people to be honest. But that broker he's been dealing with, *Khemlani* . . . my God, what a con man.' Whitlam's expression changed in an instant from irritated to puzzled. 'Rex told me it was you who introduced him to Khemlani. How did that come about?'

Out of sight, Martindale's hands tightened around the armrests of the chair. 'The University used him to raise money for a new department on Middle Eastern studies, and I met him once as part of the negotiations. He seemed okay to me and I happened to mention him to Clyde Cameron. It was Clyde who introduced Khemlani to Rex, not me.'

Whitlam let out a deflating sigh and said, 'Well . . . what's done is done. We still need a loan.'

'Do you want me to have a go at raising funds?' Martindale asked. The question echoed in his head as though uttered in a cavernous underground hole.

Whitlam's frown lifted to a grin. 'I was going to give the job to Hayden but, to be honest, I was rather hoping you'd volunteer. The job's yours if you're sure you want it.'

'I'm sure.' Martindale replied with a generous voice, though his mouth was drier than the Nullarbor.

'You'll have to move quickly, though,' Whitlam said.

'I understand.'

'We don't need Executive approval for anything up to five hundred million, so that's your immediate target. If Fraser carries through with his threat, it will be enough to continue existing projects and pay everyone's wages until Christmas. We'll need four billion in total to accomplish all our energy plans.'

'Four *billion*?'

Whitlam gave a firm nod. 'A letter of authority will be ready for you on your return from Perth. Forget the Middle East and go back to our traditional partners for the loan. Try London first.'

'All right, I will.'

'I appreciate you doing this, George. Good luck in Perth.'

*

Martindale tapped on Mrs Henderson's open door and walked in. 'Any luck with Murdoch?'

From behind her desk, she replied, 'His driver will pick you up from here at ten in the morning. You should be in Perth by four.'

He nodded a thank you and said, with a deadpan face, 'I'm going for Kate's funeral.'

'Yes . . . I thought it might be for that. We got to chatting once when you were with the PM, and Kate told me all her family lived in Perth.' Mrs Henderson looked away and placed a document in the out-tray. Meeting his eyes again, she gave the same rounded smile she always gave. 'I hope it all goes well, George.'

*

Martindale tried to order his thoughts but they always came around to Kate. Was she murdered? What did she know? The skin on his neck prickled; his breath shortened. He hoped his trip to Perth would yield some answers. For now, he needed to get his hands on her diary.

Before leaving work, Martindale spent forty minutes searching through the government archives for material on Dr Jim Cairns. He wasn't looking for anything in particular, just sufficient bulk to create a plausible-looking dossier. A meticulous cross-referenced system of index cards, plus the help of an eager young clerk, made his job easy. He bundled the documents together and put them in a lime-green cardboard sleeve, the type Kate used for ongoing projects. As a final touch, he scrawled a few small birds in flight across its front cover.

11. Kate's office

Armed with "Kate's" green file, Martindale arrived at the Sydney Building in central Canberra—the regional headquarters of Nine News—at the pre-arranged time of four o'clock.

Howard Rose breezed into the lobby at ten past the hour and marched across to greet Martindale. 'Sorry to have kept you waiting, Professor.'

'That's okay, Howard. I was just admiring the architecture.'

They shook hands.

'Quite special, isn't it?' Rose said, all smiles and chest puffed as though he had designed the building himself. 'John Sulman designed it during his Florentine phase. You can see the influence of Brunelleschi.'

'Is that right?' Martindale replied. 'It looks a little like London's Regent Arcade to me.'

With a noticeable frown, Rose extended his arm towards the far stairwell. 'Perhaps we should go straight through to my office?'

They walked up one flight of stairs and down a neon-lit corridor lined on either side with doors of frosted glass.

Kate's office was halfway along, facing the men's toilet and the only one with its door closed. Martindale slowed his pace as he went by. Maybe he should keep it simple and ask to have a look inside? A final farewell to Kate, alone?

Rose's office was at the end of the corridor. They entered and sat on opposite sides of a tidy desk. Martindale spoke first.

'I appreciate you seeing me at short notice.'

'Not at all,' Rose replied. 'First, let me say how sorry I am about Kate. I understand she was a close friend of yours.'

'Yes, thanks. It felt odd walking past her office just then.'

'I'm sure it did. It is also odd that intelligence officers from the DSD searched her office shortly after she died.'

Martindale felt the hairs on the nape of his neck rise up. Had he understood Rose correctly? 'The Defence Signals Directorate?' he said. 'Why them?'

Rose shrugged. 'You tell me. They showed up at four in the morning when the only people here were the cleaners. A coincidence, do you think?'

'Did they take anything?

'Like what?'

'I don't know. Her notebooks?'

'Not to my knowledge,' Rose said. 'But why should you care if the DSD took any of her work?'

'I don't. I'm just curious why they came at all.'

'So are we, Mister Martindale. Indeed, we are more than a little curious about her car accident. Three of my investigators were with Kate and Fred that night at Julio's, and each one of them is quite adamant Kate never touched a drop of alcohol all evening. It's rather hard to imagine, don't you think, how someone could drive headlong into a lake after drinking nothing stronger than mineral water with a slice of lime?'

Sitting stiffly, Martindale replied, 'I spoke with the district coroner this morning. His report hasn't been officially released yet, and he wanted this to be kept confidential, but . . . there *was* alcohol in her blood.'

Other than a raised brow, Rose gave no reaction.

'Her funeral's in Perth this Thursday. I'm flying over tomorrow.'

'Planes will be grounded tomorrow,' Rose said as if catching Martindale in a lie.

'Your boss has graciously offered me a lift in his Learjet.'

'You're flying with Murdoch?' Rose's mouth curled down with the look of someone who had swallowed live maggots. 'Have fun with that.' He pulled his shirtsleeve up, fully exposing his watch as he checked the time. 'In any case, Mister Martindale, how can I help you?'

'Nothing really.' Lifting the green file off his lap, Martindale said, 'Kate left these notes on Doctor Cairns in my apartment, and I thought you might want them.' He handed the file to Rose.

Rose spied the doodles on the front cover and smiled. 'She was always drawing these little birds.' Using two fingers, he prised open the file, glimpsed inside and then laid it on the desk. 'I could have sent someone to pick this up. You didn't need to make a special trip.'

Martindale shrugged. 'This is on my way home.'

'All right, thank you.'

'You know,' Martindale said hesitantly, 'Kate was convinced the CIA set Jim up.' He waited for a reaction from Rose. When none came, he went on, 'Personally, I think Jim was more than capable of screwing things up all by himself.'

'Yes, on that we can agree.'

'So you don't think the CIA's trying to undermine Whitlam?'

'On the contrary,' Rose answered, 'I think they are knee-deep in the biggest pile of excrement imaginable. Two of my brightest and best reporters were looking into CIA activities in Australia, and now they're both dead. If it was up to Murdoch, that's where the story would end.'

'Why?' Martindale said with a frown.

'I'm sure you appreciate that our illustrious editor-in-chief played a key role in Whitlam's success.'

'Of course,' Martindale replied.

'Well, he now looks set to play a key role in *removing* Whitlam from office.'

'That's not altogether a state secret, Howard. Anyone who reads Murdoch's papers will know that.'

'I don't think too many people will know that Murdoch issued instructions to *kill* Whitlam.'

'*What*?'

'Those were his exact words in a memo sent to every newspaper and TV editor he controls.' Rose added, with a grin suitable to the passing of judgement. 'I am certain Rupert only meant it figuratively, mind, and that he doesn't actually expect us to storm Parliament House with guns blazing.'

'I had no idea he disliked Gough quite that much,' Martindale said.

'Yes. And all because the Prime Minister cancelled one of his mining projects in Western Australia.'

'Hmm . . . Gough warned me not to sit too near the exit on the way to Perth. I think he was worried I might find myself departing the plane somewhere high over Kalgoorlie.'

'Indeed, yes.' Rose's tone and facial expression gave some merit to the comic suggestion. 'You might also be interested to learn that Murdoch wants any reports of foul play by the security services to be downplayed as much as possible. He doesn't want anyone to think Whitlam's implosion is based on anything other than the government's own incompetence. No offence intended, of course.'

'None taken.'

'To be fair, I don't think Murdoch has any faith in all the CIA rumours,' Rose said. 'But I recognise that Kate did.'

'Yes, she did.'

'I trust my reporters, Mister Martindale, and if they say she didn't consume any alcohol, then she didn't. I have no intention of pulling my investigators off the tail of the CIA or ASIO.' The telephone rang but Rose continued, 'Indeed, I'll add the DSD to that list.' He gestured to the phone. 'Sorry, do you mind?'

'Go ahead,' Martindale replied. This was his chance. 'I'll just pop to the loo.'

Rose picked up the phone, covered the mouthpiece with his hand and said, 'Down the corridor, on your right.'

*

The corridor was bare and Kate's office door was unlocked. Without a second thought, Martindale entered and shut the door, crossed over to her desk and opened each drawer. They were all empty.

A lone filing cabinet stood beside the desk. He skimmed through each drawer, but all he found was a wealth of reference documents and transcripts from past television broadcasts.

He turned and scanned the room: a glass table and sofa on one side, and a tall laminate bookcase on the other. The bookcase was a chaotic display of videotapes, magazines and newspapers. But no books. And no diary. A few Polaroid snaps—one of Kate— were propped up against the clutter.

A mottled figure appeared through the frosted glass door. Martindale froze. What madness was he chasing? The figure slipped away. He went on.

Looking down, he spotted Kate's briefcase under the desk. He pulled it out, snapped it open and found it empty. 'Bastards!'

Stooping to replace the case, his eyes hit on Kate's desk pad and the unmistakable sketch of a sheep lurking in the mess of notes and scribbles. 'Jesus,' he breathed. Too dense to read at a glance, he pinched the far corner of the top sheet and was about to tear it off when he heard Rose talking in the hallway.

He watched the door. No shadow was visible behind the glass but he knew Rose was near. He braced the desk pad with one hand and ripped off the sheet with the other. Roughly folded, he forced it into his trouser pocket.

The handle of the door rotated down.

Martindale rushed to the bookcase and snatched the Polaroid of Kate.

Rose entered with a compelling frown and said, 'You really shouldn't be in here.'

'Yes, sorry.'

Rose's eyes darted about the room.

'I was heading back when I peeked into Kate's office and saw this.' Martindale held out the Polaroid. 'You don't mind if I keep it, do you?'

'I don't see why not, but . . . .' Rose moved closer. 'Mister Martindale, please tell me why you—'

'I better get going, Howard. It's much later than I realised. Thanks for the photo.'

They shook hands, then Martindale was gone.

*

Martindale spent an hour at his kitchen table dissecting Kate's scribbled writings. They were untidy and barely legible but not, as he first thought, randomly arranged. The top right corner of the sheet detailed her social life—dinner dates, the cinema, Julio's—with office duties and meetings listed below. The entire left side was dedicated to interviews and outside broadcasts. Only the contact details of a bowling alley and Kate's sketch of a sheep were alien, both located at the centre. Two arrows radiated upwards from the sheep's stomach, one pointing to *"CIA"* and the other to *"NUGAN-HAND BANK"*. 'N-H,' he said to himself.

He showered and spent a shiftless twenty minutes packing for Perth, juggling the only tangible clue on offer. Was the Nugan-Hand Bank involved with the CIA? Could he risk snooping on the bank himself?

Just after ten, Martindale telephoned his research student, Geoffrey Palmer. 'Sorry to call you so late at home, Geoff, but I have a favour to ask.'

12. Black Mountain Tower

The American owned and built *Joint Defence Space Research Facility* was located in rugged outback, twelve miles south-west of Alice Springs. Its first director, Richard Stallings, had retired on the grounds of ill health. His successor, Commander James Farnsworth, took charge in January 1974.

The residents of Alice Springs had mixed feelings about the American invasion of their town. While shop owners welcomed the influx of cash, there remained an undercurrent of suspicion about what lay hidden in the nearby desert. A wall of burly soldiers met any curiosity seekers, with only one resident ever claiming to have broken through the barrier. Billy Anderson, a local prospector, boasted he had photographs of golf-ball-like structures in the wilderness, some as tall as a ten-storey building. Anderson disappeared the day after his boast.

Wednesday 9 July, Alice Springs

Commander Farnsworth was a big man. Everything about him was big: His voice. His stomach. His hands. His nose. Even his hair—thick and black, swept back from his forehead in one long wave and cemented in place with a generous scoop of Brylcreem. Prior to his appointment as Director, he had spent two decades in Washington D.C. working for the Office of Naval Intelligence. An ill-timed explosion during his first week of training left him stone-deaf in one ear. He was married to Jane, with no children, and lived in suburban Alice Springs.

At eight o'clock that Wednesday morning, dressed in pajamas, Farnsworth headed down the hallway to the bathroom with a two-day-old copy of the *Washington Post* tucked under his arm. He walked right by the ringing telephone.

Jane answered the phone. 'Wait, Jim,' she called. 'It's for you.'

'Who is it?'

'Jon Fortescue.'

'Tell him I'll be there at nine.'

'He says it's urgent.'

'Oh, for Christ's sake.' Farnsworth marched back and snatched the receiver from his wife's outstretched hand. 'Can't this wait, Fortescue?' he said, shifting his weight from one foot to the other while eyeing the open bathroom door. Listening, his newspaper fell to the floor and he stopped moving. 'When did this happen?' His grip on the phone tightened as he hung on.

'How the hell did Martindale find out about Nugan-Hand?' Farnsworth's grip grew tighter still. 'What do you mean Martindale doesn't know anything? He must know something or he wouldn't be asking Palmer to help him. And why *is* he asking Palmer?' He listened for a long moment before interrupting with loud instructions. 'All right, damn it, this is what you do. First, get a tail on Martindale while he's in Perth. Next, I want Palmer at Merino ASAP. His background is too perfect for my liking, and I want to meet him face-to-face. I certainly don't want him left in Canberra snooping around Nugan-Hand on his own. Be sure to get someone reliable to bring him in.' He waited for the reply, cradling his full belly with the palm of his hand.

'Scott Williams!' Farnsworth yelled. 'Christ almighty, Fortescue, I don't want the boy killed.'

Heeding the reply, Farnsworth gave another look to the bathroom. 'Okay, okay,' he said impatiently. 'Then tell Williams to shift his ass down to Canberra and be on the viewing platform of Black Mountain Tower by two o'clock. Someone will meet him there with further instructions. I'll phone Palmer myself, but I want you to prepare a dossier on Nugan-Hand for him. Make it plausible—a solid merchant bank, helping Australians, that sort of crap. And be sure to hide any connections to the Cayman Islands. I'll be there at nine.' Farnsworth dropped the handset back on its base and, leaving the newspaper behind, scrambled down the hall.

13. Where's Alice?

That same morning, Canberra

Palmer was somewhere between dreams and reality when he tuned in to a bell ringing. He thrust his arm from beneath the bed covers to silence the alarm clock.

The telephone kept on ringing.

'Oh, shit!'

He jumped out of bed and bolted to the sitting room, its heavy curtains drawn against the morning sun. Breathless, he snatched at the phone. 'Hello.'

'Palmer?' came the response, loud enough to cause physical pain.

Palmer jerked the receiver away as the familiar bark of Commander Farnsworth speared his hazy head. He brought it back as near as he dared and answered, 'Morning, sir.'

'Activate scramble mode.'

Palmer did so.

'I didn't wake you, did I, son?'

'No, sir.' Palmer squinted at a clock on the far wall. Through the darkness he could just make out it was nine fifteen. 'I've been working on my thesis.' He rolled his eyes at his own feeble excuse for lazing in bed.

'I'm glad to see you're getting the most out of your cover.'

'Yes, sir.' He edged back one curtain.

'If you can drag yourself away from your thesis,' Farnsworth said, 'I want you here at Merino.'

'Where is—'

'There's a flight leaving Canberra for Alice at noon tomorrow. It's never full, so you won't have any trouble getting a seat.'

'Yes, sir, but—'

'Another agent will be travelling with you—Scott Williams. Someone will contact you later with more details. Understood?'

'Yes. But Professor Martindale has asked me to—'

'We'll brief you on the Nugan-Hand Bank when you get here.'

Palmer's eyes widened and he felt compelled to sneak a look over his shoulder.

'Are you there, Palmer?'

'What about the strike?'

'What strike?' Farnsworth asked.

'The airlines went on strike last night.'

'Oh, Christ, I forgot. Well . . . you can drive, can't you?'

'Sure.'

'Good. I'll have a car delivered to you at seven in the morning. That's not too early for you, is it, son?'

'No, Commander.'

'I want you here Saturday at the latest.'

'Umm . . . .'

'Now what's the matter?' Farnsworth said.

'I don't know where Merino is.'

'Our cars are fitted with shortwave radio. Just call in when you're near Alice.'

'Where's Alice?'

'Right in the centre.'

'The centre of what?'

'Jesus Christ, Palmer. Australia!'

'Oh, you mean Alice Springs.'

'Yes, son. The base is a few miles south of there. Provided you don't hit anything, it will only take a couple of days.'

'Hit anything?'

'Kangaroos. They're everywhere out here.'

'I've never seen—'

'I'll expect you at midday on Saturday. Take plenty of water with you.'

'Okay, I—' The dial tone rang clear. Palmer put the phone down and said, 'Thanks for the advice . . . *sir*.'

14. The Englishman

Later that day, Canberra

Scott Williams was convinced he could see better with blue-tinted lenses. They darkened in the sun, though not enough to conceal that one eye refused to look in the same direction as the other. And his good eye, if that's what it was, jittered in its socket like an overloaded washing machine. His unruly blond hair and prominent beak added to his unfortunate appearance.

At forty-two, Williams had been in the employ of the CIA for almost half his life. For the past three months he had been working undercover in Sydney promoting labour unrest as a member of the Ship Painters' and Dockers' Union, a task made easier by the fact that the Union's work was equally divided between ships and organised crime.

Driving non-stop from Sydney, he reached Black Mountain Tower on the dot of two o'clock and caught the express lift to the observation platform. Shielding his eyes from the sun's reflection in the tower's glassy metal structure, Williams weaved his way around the deck, past a flock of primary school children and a few camera-laden tourists.

A suited man with a head of hair more white than grey stood alone at the eastern edge of the platform. He appeared unremarkable except for his bushy, black eyebrows. From a distance, they resembled a pair of hairy caterpillars.

Williams approached him.

Standing four feet apart, each man looked out over Lake Burley Griffin. The suited man spoke first.

'The water level looks quite low for this time of year.' The accent was English, falling somewhere between royalty and a television newsreader of the 1950s.

'It's not a natural lake,' came the reply.

With the ritual of swapping agreed verse completed, they each took a step closer to one another. Both maintained their gaze on the lake.

'I have booked you into Hotel Canberra for tonight,' the Englishman said. 'Room 213. It is quite nice for an Australian hotel. You should be comfortable there.'

'Why am I here?'

'Blunt and to the point, eh?' The Englishman's lips upturned in approval. 'I have a babysitting job for you.'

Williams sighed and lowered his head.

'Not impressed, I see.' The Englishman glimpsed over his shoulder. 'Then I suggest you listen carefully.'

Williams took off his glasses and rubbed his eyes. He said nothing.

'The target's name is Geoffrey Palmer,' the Englishman continued. 'He's one of your lot, working undercover as a Fulbright Scholar in Parliament House. You are to accompany him to see Commander Farnsworth.'

'At Merino?' Williams replaced his glasses.

'Yes.'

'That's over a thousand miles away.'

'One and a half thousand, I believe,' the Englishman answered. 'Rather a big country, isn't? One might say, unnecessarily large.'

'Yeah, I get the point.'

'And you will have to drive, of course.'

'Are you kidding me?'

'Last night's airline stoppage went ahead as planned. Aren't you pleased?'

Williams's mouth puckered into a tight ball of flesh. After a fleeting moan of consent, he asked, 'What's the deal with Palmer?'

'He has acquired some information that might cause embarrassment if it gets out.'

'You don't trust him?'

'No, we don't, but he is important to us. Palmer works with George Martindale. He's the Prime Minister's—'

'I know who Martindale is.'

'Good. Then you understand the situation.'

'I might if you tell me what's going on.'

The Englishman plucked a packet of *Benson & Hedges* and a lighter from inside his coat. 'Cigarette?'

Williams shook his head.

'I'm told you're quite thorough in your work,' the Englishman said. 'He paused to light the cigarette. 'I trust that is correct.'

There was no response.

'Farnsworth will brief you, of course, but I can tell you this much.' The Englishman took a drag and blew the smoke skywards, scanning the area again. No one was nearby. 'We are finished with Cairns. Now we have to deal with the Prime Minister. One way or another, Whitlam must be out of office before December.' After one more drag, he discarded the cigarette and ground it into the deck with his heal.

With a nod to the flattened butt end, Williams asked, 'Is that what you have in store for Whitlam?'

The question was ignored. 'All you need to know at this stage,' the Englishman said, 'is that Kissinger believes Whitlam to be a significant security threat.' He paused before adding, 'I have to admit, he is somewhat of a loose cannon.'

'Who, Whitlam or Kissinger?'

'Very funny,' came the straight-faced reply. 'Whitlam has threatened to close down Merino. It may well be an empty gesture on his part but we are not taking any chances.'

'Why December?' Williams asked.

'The agreement covering Merino's renewal is due then. If we can destabilise the government with labour unrest and strikes, we may yet force an early election. Frankly, though, time is fast running out for that approach. That is why we are setting up a new task group, to hurry things up and oversee some additional operations.' He faced Williams and stated, 'You're in it.'

Williams held the Englishman's eyes for a moment and answered, with the smallest of nods, 'Go on.'

'The group will remain ultra-secret, and isolated from the CIA. That was Kissinger's idea—a safeguard for himself and the boys at Langley should everything go belly-up. For operational cover, the Nugan-Hand Bank will be used. The first meeting will take place this Saturday at Merino. Be there by midday.'

'Who else is in it?'

'You will be briefed on Saturday,' the Englishman replied, his focus drawn to a rowdy group of schoolchildren playing ten feet away.

'Tell me about Palmer,' Williams said.

'To position an agent close to Whitlam, we baited Martindale with a research student. Palmer was new to the agency but the obvious choice. He was the right age, a Yale graduate, top of the class in—'

'Benjamin!' screeched a schoolteacher. 'Leave Jemima alone and come here at once.' The young boy and a few of his friends were close by, pinning the two agents against the glass barrier at the deck's edge.

'Shall we move on,' the Englishman said, already forcing one child aside with his arm.

They walked clockwise around the tower. On reaching the lift, the Englishman pressed the call button. 'Palmer will be in the lobby of Hotel Canberra at nine tomorrow morning. He is about your height, dark hair, twenty-six and skinny as a rake. Use the same approach greeting.'

'Is that it?'

'He will have an agency car with him.'

'I have a car.'

'Leave it at the hotel and use Palmer's.'

The lift bobbed up. It was empty and Williams stepped in.

The Englishman stayed on deck. A moment before the doors slid together, he said, 'Have a pleasant journey.'

15. Wrong side

The following morning

Geoffrey Palmer stood at the rear of Hotel Canberra's lobby with his head buried in an unfolded map of the Australian highways. Dressed in blue jeans, T-shirt and a thin woollen jumper, he had a Nikon camera with telephoto lens hanging around his neck and a battered grey rucksack by his side. He did not see Williams approach.

'Palmer?'

Palmer flinched, splitting the map a few inches down its central fold. The person standing before him matched the description he had been given, and he began, 'The water in the lake—'

'Yeah, yeah, it's not a natural lake.'

Palmer buried his impulse to look in the direction of the lobby, where Williams' dodgy left eye was pointed. 'Good morning, sir,' he said.

'You know where to go, then,' Williams said with a nod to the map.

'Yes, I think so. We head west for about eight hundred miles to Port Augusta, and then north along the Stuart Highway for another eight hundred. Easy enough, but it's a long way.'

'You don't say.' Williams' good eye fixed on Palmer's camera. 'We're not going on a sightseeing trip.'

'Sorry?'

'What's with the camera?'

Palmer wrapped his fingers around the long lens. 'It's a hobby of mine to photograph barren scenes, and I was hoping to get a few shots around Ayers Rock. Maybe we could—'

'Tell me later, kid. I need to check out of this place.'

'Sure . . . . Our car is out front, by the way. They've given us an automatic with air conditioning, so it should—'

Williams held out his hand. 'Keys.'

'I thought I was driving.'

'I'm driving,' Williams stated.

After a brief pause, Palmer dragged the keys from his jeans and handed them over.

Williams pocketed the keys and said, 'I'll see you outside.' He then turned and walked to the checkout desk.

Palmer kept his mouth tight shut as he watched Williams walk away. Why did he have to drive sixteen hundred miles into a baking hot wasteland with a miserable, monosyllabic one-eyed git?

'Where's the car?' Williams asked.

Palmer gestured to a dark blue Ford sedan parked on the far side of the road and immediately stepped off the kerb, looking to his left.

Williams grabbed him by the scruff of his collar and held him up.

'Hey!' Palmer yelled as the Number Sixty-Six bus to Queanbeyan rolled by, giving a nudge to his rucksack.

'You do understand,' Williams said with the casual charm of a rattlesnake, 'that they drive on the wrong side of the road in this country?'

'Sorry,' Palmer said. His tone and look were that of a scolded child. 'I'm always doing that.'

'You owe me one, kid. Let's go.'

16. Murdoch

Later that same day

Rupert Murdoch tapped Martindale's arm and said, pointing out the window of his Learjet, 'That's Kalgoorlie down there. Hell of a lot more to be found in those mines, I can tell you.'

Martindale returned a civil nod. Was the time up for cordial conversation? Murdoch had been the perfect host during the flight, happy it seemed to leave politics behind and spend the journey discussing sports, movies, the theatre and his newspapers, especially a recent acquisition called *News of the World*. But mining rights, Martindale was only too aware, were a sore point.

'I don't think your boss,' Murdoch went on, 'has the slightest notion of how much money is buried in the ground of this state. This could be the richest place on the planet if Whitlam would allow private enterprise a little freedom.'

'Are you talking about coal mining in particular, Rupert, or the whole Aboriginal Land Rights Commission?'

Murdoch ignored the question and said, 'If it wasn't for me, Whitlam wouldn't even be in power.'

If it wasn't for you, Martindale thought, Whitlam might stay in power. 'I'm sure Gough appreciates everything you've done for him, Rupert.'

'That's not how it looks to me. Where's my reward? I was in line for the post of High Commissioner to London. Did he tell you that?'

'Yes, but I don't think Gough was keen on the idea of your empire being run from the commissioner's official residence.'

Murdoch waved the comment away. 'You might consider looking for a new job before this year is out.'

Without replying, Martindale looked back out the window and watched Kalgoorlie slide away.

*

They landed in Perth at four-thirty, the sky dark with the promise of a storm. The control tower directed the pilot to a hangar beside the northern edge of the airport terminal.

A black Ford LTD with personalised number plate RM1 was waiting by the hanger's entrance. A uniformed chauffeur stood by the driver's door. A young woman, with a stiff back and an even stiffer smile, stood beside the front passenger's door.

Murdoch reverted to host-mode as they approached the car. With an open hand on Martindale's back, he said. 'Let me give you a ride into Perth.'

'Thanks, Rupert, but it's no problem catching a taxi straight to the hotel.'

'Are you sure?'

'Yes.'

'Okay, George, if that's what you want.'

The two men stopped short of the car.

The young woman moved forward a pace. 'Good afternoon, sir.'

'Hello, Cassandra.' Murdoch gave a wink to the chauffeur and then turned to face Martindale. 'If the airline strike doesn't end soon, give me a call and I'll see what I can do.'

'I will. Thank you.'

With their right hands locked together, Murdoch braced his left hand against Martindale's shoulder and squeezed. Martindale did the same. They could have passed for lifelong friends. They weren't.

17. The mother

L ake Monger please,' Martindale said on stepping into the taxi.

The driver reset the flag fall meter, signalled his destination to a chirpy voice on the shortwave radio and pulled away from the kerb. 'First time to Perth?' he asked.

'Yes,' Martindale replied. Why did he lie?

'I'd keep well away from those black swans at the lake. They might look friendly enough, but they'll take your hand off given half a chance.'

'So I hear.' Martindale let his head flop back against the seat, eyes closed.

The driver witnessed this in the rear-view mirror and drove on in silence.

On hearing the tires thump against the rubber joints in the Causeway Bridge, Martindale opened his eyes. The city was dead ahead. A firm westerly skimmed the surface of the Swan River, scattering white tips of foam as far as he could see. A few spots of rain and a belly-growl of thunder hinted at what was to come. He exhaled with a loud sigh.

'Are you all right, mate?' the driver asked, eyeing the rear-view.

His mind adrift, Martindale did not respond.

*

The Eucalyptus and Cedar trees that lined much of the lake danced in tune with the wind, their high tips only visible in outline against the fading light. The area was all but deserted. Two teenage boys struggled to drag their dinghy to shore. A scraggy Border collie rummaged through the overspill from a rubbish bin. No swans were present, though the occasional squawk filtered over from the far side of the lake.

Without an address, Martindale focused on what to look for. Kate had painted an idyllic picture of her childhood home—a double-fronted weatherboard house with a bright red door, bullnose verandas to the front and sides, a corrugated iron roof and a white picket fence. Images of the house had invaded his sleep several times since her death.

Carrying a small overnight case, Martindale walked to the end of a long wooden pier that jutted into the water. His eyes traced the neat row of tall trees around the park to a clearing in the west, where individual homes crowned a small hill. What was the name that the coroner gave . . . Lakeview? He nodded. It was a long shot, of course, but worth a try. He walked back down the pier and headed west out of the reserve. A few minutes later, near the crest of the hill, Martindale was standing opposite the very image of the house Kate had planted in his mind.

The wind was blowing in all directions now. In the short distance from the pavement to the steps of the veranda, scattered spots of rain became a shower of marble-sized pellets.

Sheltered under the awning, Martindale flicked at the water on his shoulders and patted his face dry with the sleeve of his coat. With a diligent look around, he approached the front door. The sash windows either side of it were dark. Was anybody home? There was no doorbell, only a small brass knocker behind a torn fly-wire screen. He held the screen open and knocked three times. There was no answer. He knocked twice more and then let the screen snap shut.

Moments later, the panes of frosted glass beside the door lit up and strips of neon lighting blazed across the veranda's ceiling. The door opened.

She had dark, serious eyes, and the skin beneath them was glistening in the neon brilliance.

'Missus Donahue?' he said.

'Yes.'

'I'm sorry to bother you. My name is—'

'I know who you are, Mister Martindale.' Her manner was perfunctory. Not surprised, not inviting. The fly-wire screen remained shut.

'I would have phoned first but your number is ex-directory.'

She peered over his shoulder at the heavy rain. 'Please come in,' she said, pushing the wire door open.

In the amber glow of the hallway light, she looked younger. She looked like Kate—the same round face, the same height, the same slim figure. Even her voice was similar, projecting a visceral strength that belied her sad eyes.

'I wasn't sure of your address,' Martindale said.

'Then how did you find the house?'

'Kate described it to me once. Plus I knew the name of the house and guessed it must have had a view of Lake Monger.'

She made no comment.

'Anyhow, I took a taxi here and just started looking.'

'I see.'

Her reply sounded more like a question than a statement. An awkward silence followed until Martindale broke it with, 'Kate told me how she used to play on the veranda as a little girl, watching the swans bite the tourists and steal their food.'

Mrs Donahue offered her right hand and said, 'Kate's funeral is tomorrow.'

'Yes, that's why I've come. I hope you don't mind?'

She paused as a grandfather clock, standing at the end of the hall, chimed the hour. 'I was about to make some tea. Would you like a cup?'

He could kill for a whisky. 'Tea would be great.'

She showed him through to the living room. 'Please take a seat. I'll only be a few minutes.'

Martindale sank into a well-worn armchair next to a fireplace filled with a vase of wilting lilies. He sneezed twice. A honey-coloured baby grand piano sat in the corner of the room, its closed lid sprinkled with a dozen or more framed photographs. Many more photos were on display about the room, on almost every flat surface. His curiosity settled on those over the fireplace. He recognised Kate in each one of them—as a small girl riding a bike, as a young woman riding a horse, sitting at the piano, playing under a tree, smiling, laughing. The nearest photo showed Kate at about twelve years of age, standing with her arms wrapped around a small boy. Did she have a little brother? He edged forward for a closer look. The family resemblance was unmistakable.

Sitting back, he listened to the rain slapping the iron roof, magnifying the storm outside. Three minutes went by before the living room door opened and Mrs Donahue walked in carrying a tray of tea and dried biscuits. She sat opposite Martindale and set the tray on a low table between them.

'I didn't know Kate played the piano,' he said as an opener for conversation.

'Yes, Kate loved playing.' She poured his tea.

With a glance to the mantelshelf, he asked, 'Is that her little brother?'

Mrs Donahue's hand trembled as she poured her own tea, and a few drops splashed onto the saucer. Sharp-edged patches of red skin emerged on her neck and cheeks.

The back of his neck tingled. Had he said something wrong?

'I did phone your office to tell you about the funeral arrangements,' Mrs Donahue said.

'I didn't get the message.'

'That's because I didn't leave one.' She held back a second before asking, 'How did you know when the funeral was being held?'

'I spoke with the coroner.'

'Why?' Her voice was firm, almost angry. 'Why did you do that?'

A slew of excuses filled his head, but he didn't offer one.

'Did you believe what they said on the TV?' Mrs Donahue asked. 'Because I can assure you that my daughter would not have drunk any alcohol.' She lifted her cup and saucer off the table, then promptly put them down again. 'Why did they say that? Why did they say Kate was drunk?'

'Given the circumstances,' Martindale replied, 'I suppose they assumed she must have been drinking.'

'What circumstances?'

'Kate had been at a nightclub most of the evening.'

'She never drank alcohol.'

'Well . . . .'

'Did you ever *see* her drink?'

'No,' he said quietly.

'No, because she couldn't. Kate knew it would . . . .' Mrs Donahue stopped and took two gulps of air. 'Kate knew that . . . .' She stopped again, squeezed her hands together and held the ball of matted fingers against her mouth.

'I'm sorry Missus Donahue.' His quiet acknowledgement of her distress was lost in the rain's beating noise on the iron roof.

She shook her head and placed both hands face down on her lap. 'Kate never drank because she knew it would kill her.' When the words finally came, they were flung as a blunt statement of fact.

At that moment, the front windows filled with light and a deafening clap of thunder struck their ears. The rainstorm was overhead and the commotion it brought allowed Martindale a few seconds to gather his thoughts. But it wasn't long enough and Mrs Donahue spoke first.

'She had a rare condition that made her allergic to alcohol. Did you know that?'

He gave a vague shake of his head. 'I knew she was asthmatic, though.'

'Yes, which made the problem worse. *Much* worse. Even a small amount of alcohol gave her terrible headaches—her lips and tongue would swell, she couldn't breathe. Her father had the same condition and Kate watched him die from it right here in this room.'

Martindale opened his mouth to speak but Mrs Donahue carried on.

'It was only ten days after her brother died.' A single chime filtered through the walls. It was a quarter past six. 'Drinking was the only way Max could find to numb his misery. Maybe he didn't understand . . . .' She stopped and, without warning, stood. 'Will you excuse me? I won't be a moment.'

Martindale had not heard the front door open. Listening, he could just pick out a muffled conversation followed by a door closing hard somewhere deep in the house.

Mrs Donahue re-entered the room. 'Sorry about that.' She sat halfway into the chair. 'Of course, Mister Martindale, we would be happy for you to come to the funeral.'

'Thank you.'

'But you must have known that already. You hardly needed our permission to go.'

'No, I—'

'Then please explain why you're here. You could begin by telling me why you spoke with the coroner?'

Martindale recognised the steely determination in her voice. He had heard it many times in Kate during their brief time together. 'I wanted to find out if she suffered, that was all. I thought I might cope a little better if I knew she didn't suffer.'

Mrs Donahue's eyes glassed over. 'And did she?'

He shook his head. 'Everything happened very quickly.'

'You believed the coroner.'

'Yes, of course.'

'And do you believe what they said about the crash . . . that Kate was drunk?'

He didn't speak, but nor did he look away.

'You don't, do you?' she said. 'You know it wasn't an accident?'

'I don't know that,' Martindale replied.

'Then what *do* you know?'

With a glance to the photographs over the fireplace, he said, 'I promised Kate I would follow up what she was working on.'

'And why come here to do that?'

'Kate told me she always discussed her work with you.'

'Do you honestly think she would have said more to me than to you?'

'I guess she valued your opinion as a journalist.'

'My days as a journalist were a long time ago, Mister Martindale.' A thunderclap burst through the room. The wall lights flickered, threatening to expire. 'This is about the CIA, isn't it?'

'What did Kate tell you?'

'She said they were determined to destroy Prime Minister Whitlam. I thought she was joking, but . . . .'

'The first time Kate said anything to me was the night before she died,' Martindale said. 'All I really know is that Fred Saunders was working with her.'

'Yes, and now they're *both* dead.' Mrs Donahue paused before adding, 'When they said Kate was drunk, we went straight to the police and told them about her condition. We also told them what she said about the CIA.'

He felt a flush rise from deep in his gut. 'What did they say?'

'They laughed at us. But the very next day a detective came to the house with a preliminary copy of the coroner's findings. It stated that there *was* alcohol in Kate's blood.

'She might have taken someone else's drink by mistake,' Martindale offered.

'Did Kate ever strike you as being that careless?'

'The nightclub was crowded and noisy; it would have been an easy mistake to make.'

Mrs Donahue squinted a little. 'You were there?'

'Not that night, but Julio's is always busy. It's the only club in town.'

'If there was alcohol in her blood, Mister Martindale, someone put it there.'

'What do you mean?'

'Someone could have spiked her drink.'

He had no reply, and his face gave nothing away.

A clash of pots and pans punctured their stares; her eyes flashed towards the racket.

Martindale sensed his time was almost up. 'Did she ever mention the Nugan-Hand Bank?' he asked.

'What on earth has that got to do with anything?'

'Did she mention it?'

'No.'

There was another burst of thunder, softer this time. The storm was moving away.

'What about Merino?' he asked quickly.

'Is that the name of the spy?'

'Spy?'

'Kate told me there was an agent in the government, someone close to the Prime Minister.'

His brow furrowed. 'She never said that to me,' he lied.

'That's because she thought it was you or . . . your wife.'

'*My wife?*'

'There was a rumour in the newsroom that your wife's death was somehow suspicious,' Mrs Donahue said.

The words pierced his core; his face stiffened.

'You needn't look so worried, Mister Martindale. It was before Kate met you, and it didn't take her long to realise the story was nonsense.'

Without a suitable comeback, he stroked his chin as casually as he could.

'What is Merino?' she asked.

'Kate thought it might be the codename for an American military base.'

Mrs Donahue shrugged her shoulders. 'She never mentioned the name Merino, but she did think there was some kind of secret base at Alice Springs. Could that be it?'

'Maybe.'

The noises from the kitchen grew louder. 'I must go,' she said. 'If I leave Jack on his own in the kitchen for much longer he'll burn the house down.'

'I'm sure Kate's death was an accident, Missus Donahue.' His tone was neither comforting nor convincing.

'Are you?'

'Yes . . . and one more thing. Don't go to the police again.'

'That's an odd request isn't it, given what we've just been talking about?'

'I understand how you feel, but let me do it my way or we'll never find out what happened.'

'And what is your way?'

'I'll find the truth, Missus Donahue, even it kills me.'

'That just might happen.'

*

Martindale's room at the Sheraton was like a hundred others he had slept in over the past two years, except for the view. The night's deluge had ended, and he stood gazing at the apartments of South Perth reflected in the rippled surface of the Swan River.

He took stock: Mrs Donahue knew as little as he did about the Nugan-Hand Bank. She was as suspicious of Kate's death as he was. And Merino might be near Alice Springs, if it exists at all.

The only fact Martindale knew with any certainty was that his wife's death would continue to follow him wherever he went.

18. Rocky outcrops

Saturday 12 July, Stuart Highway, Northern Territory

Driving two hundred and fifty unbroken miles from the opal-mining town of Coober Pedy, Palmer and Williams reached the northernmost edge of South Australia at midday. A small lay-by with two picnic benches and a rusted old water tank were the only features that marked their entry to the Northern Territory.

The view in front matched the one behind: an empty streak of bitumen, blurred in the heat, carving a line through a vast plain of spinifex and mulga, disappearing at the horizon beneath a cloudless blue sky. No wildlife was visible, save for the odd dead kangaroo lying splayed at the edge of the road.

His face paralysed with boredom, Williams stopped and gave the wheel to Palmer for the remainder of the journey.

An hour later, with the air conditioner switched off to stop the engine from overheating, the temperature in the car reached eighty-five. The black dashboard cooked in the sun, filling the car with the stink of heated vinyl.

Neither the heat nor rank air stopped Williams from falling asleep in the passenger's seat. He snored loudly.

Palmer fared less well. Hunched over the wheel, swiping at his windblown hair, he could not get comfortable. His T-shirt remained glued to his back with sweat, while his underwear felt like soggy sandpaper. He tugged at his jeans every few minutes and twisted back and forth in his seat, all to no avail. Eyeing the silent air conditioner, he said, 'You useless piece of shit.'

As a final effort to cool his groin, Palmer slowed to forty, pushed the driver's seat back a little and, with his left foot on the accelerator, eased his right foot out the window. A current of air ballooned the leg of his flared jeans, bringing a wave of relief so intense he almost burst out laughing. He sped on as fast as the car and his contorted shape would allow.

Passing a battered signpost for the town of Ghan, Palmer's eyes widened in anticipation of downing a long, cold glass of something. He scanned left and right for signs of life, but there were none—no houses, no shops, no garage, not even a dead kangaroo. All he saw was a lonely dirt road heading east, and he assumed the town must be located at the end of it. Should he risk a detour? They were running late for their meeting with Farnsworth, and fuel was low. He drove on.

Another car approached in the distance. Palmer welcomed the distraction until its blue checkerboard markings became visible. He clocked his speed at ninety-two, and checked the rear-view as the patrol car cruised by. 'Damn,' he said on seeing two small flashes of red. He thumped the steering wheel.

Slumped in his seat, Williams jerked at the thud and sat up. 'Ahh, fucking hell.'

'What's wrong with you?' snapped Palmer, his eyes darting between the road ahead and Williams' knotted face.

'My back . . . .' Williams squirmed to unfreeze his muscles, twisting enough to spot the flashing blue lights out the rear window. 'By the way,' he said with a quizzical look at Palmer's leg out the window, 'the cops are following.'

'Yeah, I got that.'

'They just flashed us.'

'I know!' Palmer slowed and came to a stop on the dusty red soil by the side of the road. With singular effort, he pulled his leg back into the car.

The patrol car went past and stopped ten yards in front. One officer stepped out and sauntered over to Palmer and Williams. The other officer remained behind, talking on the radio.

Stooped to peer through the driver's window, the patrolman said, 'G'day fellas.'

'Hi,' Palmer said. 'Is there a problem?'

'Could I see some identification please?'

Palmer tendered his driver's licence from California State—he had never bothered to obtain an Australian licence.

'American, eh. You're a long way from home.'

Palmer cocked an eye at the barren landscape. 'We seem to be a long way from anywhere.'

The patrolman returned the licence and said, 'I suppose you're going to that space station south of Alice.'

'That's right,' Palmer replied.

Williams twisted his head and scowled at Palmer.

'Thought so,' said the patrolman. 'Do you know where the turn-off is?'

'Sort of.'

'It's pretty hard to spot, actually. You guys keeping some aliens down there or something?'

Palmer affected a smile.

'Yeah, anyways,' said the patrolman, 'keep a lookout for a dirt track on the left past Roe Creek Bridge. About half a mile in there's a big warning sign to turn back, but I guess you guys can ignore that.'

'How far to the bridge?' Palmer asked.

'From here . . . 'bout a hundred and fifty miles, I reckon.'

'Is there any place to get some gas?'

'Petrol? No worries, mate. Erldunda's just up a way. Great café and all.'

'Okay, thanks.'

'Just keep a sharp eye out along this stretch of road, and slow down for any 'roos.'

Palmer accepted he was probably speeding and asked, 'What is the speed limit?'

'What can she do?' the patrolman said.

Not understanding the reply, Palmer repeated, 'What's the speed limit on this road?'

'The car, mate. How fast can she go?'

Palmer hesitated before replying, 'I'm not sure. Why?'

'There's no speed limit out here, mate. You go for it if you want. Just try not to hit anything.'

'Right . . . okay,' Palmer said. 'If there's nothing else, we're running—'

'Actually, there is one thing. I don't know what it's like in the States, mate, but in Australia it's against the law to operate a motor vehicle with one leg hanging out the window.'

Palmer's already flushed cheeks turned another shade deeper in colour. 'Sorry, I was hot.'

'Were ya, now? You might try a cold beer. That usually does the trick, I find.'

A mask of disbelief replaced Williams' scowl.

'You take care now, fellas, and av-a-good-weekend.' The officer gave a sharp pat to the car roof and walked back to his colleague.

Palmer and Williams watched as the patrol car made a rapid U-turn and sped south towards the state border.

'They're a funny lot, these Aussies,' Palmer said.

'Yeah . . . hilarious,' Williams replied. 'Let's go.'

Palmer gazed at the rocky outcrops of the MacDonnell Ranges in the distance, visible as a grey haze floating over the land. He drove to the base in silence.

19. Pine Gap

The guard at the outer perimeter checkpoint, dozing in the sweltering wooden hut at the end of his shift, stirred when he saw a long trail of dust in the east. Through binoculars, the guard noted the approaching car's make and model, registration, colour and number of occupants. He checked the details against the visitors list for 12 July: Geoffrey Palmer (26 yrs, 5'10", brown hair, green eyes) and Scott Williams (42 yrs, 5'11", blond hair, blue eyes), driving a blue Ford sedan (# YCW-33Z), expected at twelve hundred hours for Commander Farnsworth.

Marking their arrival time as fourteen thirty-seven, the guard sucked in a breath through rounded lips, shook his head and said, 'I wouldn't like to be in their shoes.' As the car drew near, he closed the window and kicked the door shut.

The dust trailed the car to the wooden barrier gates, smothering both the car and the hut in a dense cloud of fine red powder—a powder that clogged lungs, stained clothes, irritated eyes and literally caked your body when combined with sweat.

The sedan's horn beeped twice in quick succession.

'Hold your horses there, buddy,' the guard said to himself as he clipped the visitors' sheet to a foolscap board. When the red mist was all but gone, he left the hut and strolled over to the passenger's side door. 'Your names, please?'

'Scott Williams.'

'Geoff Palmer.'

He ticked each name. 'Please open the trunk.'

Palmer pulled the latch under the dashboard.

The guard walked to the rear of the car, lifted the trunk lid and noted one rucksack and one small suitcase. He examined the spare tyre compartment. All in order, he secured the trunk, added one more tick to the sheet and went back to the passenger's door. 'Please drive on to the next checkpoint.'

Parked inside the prison-like entrance gates, Palmer and Williams were escorted on foot to an office by the men's sleeping quarters, where they each received a visitor's ID badge and meal coupons for two days. Formalities completed, they were led on a ten-minute walk to the classified Communications Centre on the northern edge of the compound, past an open-air swimming pool and across the compound's solitary patch of green lawn. The day shift had another hour to run and the base appeared deserted, with nothing to hear except for a few geckos scurrying about.

The Communications Centre lay sandwiched between two silvery-white radomes that protected the enclosed antennae against wind and rain and hid their operational elements from inquisitive eyes. There were three more radomes at the base and eighteen single-storey buildings. Each building was made of concrete-block, painted white to help insulate it against the bitter heat. Two chain-linked fences surrounded the compound, providing a seven-square-mile exclusion zone. The outer fence discouraged most uninvited visitors. The inner fence, topped with barbed wire and patrolled twenty-four hours a day, effectively stopped all challenges to the base. Beyond the perimeter fencing were uninterrupted views across the red desert to the east and west. The

MacDonnell Ranges were visible to the north and south. The only road to the base was unsealed, making it impossible for anyone to approach by car unnoticed. No aircraft were permitted to fly within a radius of three miles.

Jonathan Fortescue greeted the men at the Centre's entrance. An athletic man in his mid-thirties, Fortescue had trained as a cryptanalyst with the US Military Intelligence Corps. He gave a tame smile to Williams and said, 'Long time, no see.'

Williams returned a mock salute with two pointed fingers.

'We need to hurry,' Fortescue said. 'The Commander's waiting and he's not a patient man.' He shook hands with Palmer and then led them both inside.

The Centre's lobby, decorated with thick navy-blue carpet and wood-panelled walls, was in sharp contrast to the drabness of its exterior. Portraits of President Gerald Ford and Dr Henry Kissinger dominated the left wall; flags of the United States and the Central Intelligence Agency dominated the right.

They walked down a narrow corridor past several office doors, some half open. From one room came the sound of quiet laughter, from another the buzz of discussion, and from another still the mechanical song of a dot matrix printer. At the corridor's end, Fortescue tapped a five-digit code into a keypad for entry to the Operations Floor.

The heart of the building was a blacked-out room the size of two tennis courts laid end-to-end, illuminated by desk lamps, computer screens and wall lights, the whole soaked in a mist of tobacco smoke. All the analysts were dressed in short-sleeve, open-neck shirts, with many sporting a bulky headset with microphone attachment. The noise of several IBM mainframes echoed off the walls and low-set ceiling.

Painted signs above various work areas indicated the type of activities performed. Palmer locked his glare on a sign near the centre of the room that read *Soviet Missile Tracking Station*.

Fortescue led them to a door at the far end of the room. 'This is the Commander's office.' He gave two brisk knocks, pulled the door open and stood aside for them to enter. 'Good luck, guys.'

The guarded room on the other side of the Operations Floor was the *Signals Analysis and Processing Office*. To everyone on the base, it was simply "the black vault". As Fortescue approached, the guard swung open the heavy metal door. A whoosh of cold air greeted them and Fortescue stepped inside. The door closed behind him.

The windowless room measured ten by fifteen feet and, although air-conditioned, stank like a smokers den. Mike Brady, a junior cypher clerk nearing the end of his shift, was dozing over a desk crowded with papers, an assortment of coffee mugs and two computer monitors. One monitor connected with several mainframes in the central communications area, while the other served a dedicated—and noisy—mainframe in the room. Also in the room were three metal filing cabinets, a reel-to-reel tape machine, an industrial shredder and a six-numbered combination lock safe. A narrow strip down the long axis of the room was the only free space, monitored continuously by a wide-angle video camera mounted on the ceiling.

'Mike,' Fortescue called.

Brady jerked upright and swung around in his chair. 'Sir,' he said.

'Is Martindale back yet?' Fortescue asked.

'Yes, he was on the morning flight to Sydney. I've already informed the Commander.'

Pushing one mug aside, Fortescue leaned against the desk. 'Did he talk to Mrs Donahue again?'

'Only for a couple of minutes after the funeral. Then he went back to his room at the Sheraton.'

'Good. Are the wiretaps in her house all set?'

Brady nodded and said, 'We've already got a recording.' He gripped a bulky manila folder containing transcripts of conversations recorded over the last few hours and handed it to Fortescue. 'Her file's about half-way down.'

'Anything else?'

'Yeah,' Brady said with a chuckle. 'Jimmy Hoffa's not long for this world.'

'Are you serious?'

Brady dipped his head to the folder and said, 'It's on top.'

Fortescue lifted the cover and began reading: *Hoffa's attempts to regain power in Teamster's threaten Lombardi and Moretti families' control of Union funds. His removal now agreed. Hit arranged at Machus Red Fox Restaurant, Bloomfield, Detroit.* 'Well, well,' he said. 'I'll give it to Jenkins, though I doubt he'll do anything to stop it.' He smoothed the cover flat. 'Anything from Canberra?'

'Just more sweet honey calls from Doctor Cairns to Junie Morosi.'

'We don't have to worry about Cairns anymore.'

Brady broke eye contact to read a fresh signal on the monitor.

'Take it if you need to,' Fortescue said.

Lifting his headset to one ear, Brady listened for a few seconds. 'It's nothing.' He tapped the keyboard and the screen cleared.

'We've got a wiretap in the apartment of Martindale's son now,' Fortescue said. 'His name is Timothy, and we need to keep a watch on him as well.'

Though no new signal was apparent, Brady looked at the monitor again. He said nothing.

'Is something wrong?' Fortescue asked.

After an awkward delay, Brady faced Fortescue head-on and said, 'I don't get it.'

'You don't get what?'

'What's Martindale's son got to do with anything?'

'We have our orders, Mike, and we follow them.'

'I guess.' Brady's lips levelled in a taut, straight line.

'Spit it out, Mike.'

'When you listen in on someone's life day and night, you get to know them pretty well. They wake up and I'm there. They go to sleep and I'm there. Then some of them finish up . . . dead. It's hard sometimes, that's all.'

'I think you've been stuck in this room too long, Mike. Are you up for a job rotation soon?'

'End of next week.'

'Good.' Fortescue glanced at a wall clock above the door. 'Go and get some rest. I'll take over until the next shift—I have to hang around here in any case.'

'Okay . . . thanks.' Brady stood and, without any belongings to collect, squeezed past Fortescue and left immediately.

Fortescue sat in Brady's chair, unplugged the headset and turned up the volume on both monitors. He leafed through the folder transcripts, stopping at the single-page script of a conversation between Mrs Margaret Donahue and Inspector Harry O'Brien. He pulled it from the file, read it, then folded it in two and placed it in a plain white envelope. He marked the front, in red pen, "CONFIDENTIAL: For Comm. F".

20. Lamingtons

The door to Farnsworth's inner office flew open and the white-haired Englishman from Canberra walked out, red-faced and muttering to himself.

Palmer and Williams were sitting on Mrs Gibson's sofa. The Englishman left without acknowledging either of them.

'When did *he* get here?' Williams asked.

'Two days ago,' Mrs Gibson answered, typing with vigour.

'He flew here?'

'Yes.' She stopped typing and looked up. 'By private charter.'

Williams clenched his jaw tight enough to make a muscle in his cheek twitch. 'We drove for three days while mister high and mighty—'

'You can go in now, gentlemen. The Commander's expecting you.'

As they crossed to the inner office, Williams carried on spouting, his words distorting into a series of grunts and whines.

Palmer knocked on the door. There was no answer.

'Go on in,' Mrs Gibson said. 'Between you and me, he's a bit hard of hearing.'

They entered, closed the door and stood by it.

Farnsworth, facing away from the door, was standing behind his desk leafing through an open filing cabinet.

'Good afternoon, sir,' Palmer said.

Farnsworth pulled a record from the middle drawer and began reading it.

Palmer shot a glance at Williams, waited a few seconds longer and then shrieked, 'GOOD AFTERNOON, SIR.'

Farnsworth lurched forward, shunting the drawer with his paunch. Twisting around, he said, '*Christ*, man, I'm not completely deaf.'

'Sorry, sir,' Palmer said.

Farnsworth aimed his backside at the chair by the desk and more or less fell into it. 'Sit down, both of you.' He acknowledged Williams with a pithy grunt.

Williams returned the same.

'You're Palmer, I assume.' Farnsworth said.

'Yes, sir.'

'You look hot. Did you take some water with you?'

'We did. It was—'

'Why were you stopped by the police?'

Palmer's jaw plummeted. How in blazes did he know that? He looked at Williams for support, though he may well have been ogling a fossilised tree trunk.

'*Well*?' Farnsworth demanded.

'I'm not sure,' Palmer replied.

'What do you mean you're not sure?'

'It might have been for my leg.'

'What's wrong with your leg?'

'It was hanging out the window.'

Farnsworth's head tilted back and his eyebrows narrowed.

'I was hot, sir,' Palmer offered.

'And your leg was particularly hot, was it?'

'Not exactly,' he replied slowly. 'The thing is—'

'Forget it.' Farnsworth opened a drawer of his desk and pulled out a slim dossier. 'This is for you,' he said, handing it to Palmer. 'It has everything you need to know about Nugan-Hand, and should be more than enough to satisfy Martindale's apparent curiosity. Take it with you, read it carefully and meet me back here at six. If you have any questions, ask me then. Your flight back to Canberra leaves at seven thirty.'

'Tonight?' Palmer's green eyes blazed with disbelief, peppered with anger.

'Yes.'

'But I only just got here.'

'Martindale's in Canberra now, so I want you back there ASAP. Got it?'

'I was hoping I'd get some time to photograph Ayres Rock.'

'We didn't bring you here for a holiday, son.'

'No, sir,' Palmer said quietly. Instead, he had slogged a thousand miles through the boondocks for a fucking bit of paper!

'Missus Gibson will tell where you can get a bite to eat before you leave,' Farnsworth offered.

'Is that it?' Palmer said without any trace of reverence in his voice.

Farnsworth rocked his head from side to side, cracking his neck. 'Fortescue's going to give you a tour of the base when we're done. Pay close attention, because you need to understand just how important Merino is to our defence programme.'

'You can track Russian missiles?' Palmer said.

'That's right, son. We can follow everything those damn Russians are doing. With the push of a button, we can command our nuclear subs and naval groups all over the world. But that idiot Whitlam is threatening to pull the plug on us. We *cannot* let that happen. Did you know that Whitlam is the only Australian prime minister to visit Moscow?'

Palmer shook his head.

'I tell you, Whitlam's a goddam communist. And so is that Attorney-General of his, Lionel Murphey. For Christ's sake, Murphey even married a Russian. We must keep on top of this government, son. Whitlam discusses everything with Martindale, and that's where you come in. You need to stick like glue to Martindale and find out whatever you can. Understood?'

Palmer gave a nod firm enough to signal his obedience and, he hoped, end the history lecture.

'And while you're at it,' Farnsworth added, 'keep your ears peeled for any talk about uranium.'

'What kind of talk?'

'It doesn't matter what kind of talk, just report anything you hear. But *don't* go snooping around the Nugan-Hand Bank. Everything you need to know is in that file. Write out the details in your own hand and give it to Martindale as your report.'

'What's so important about a bank?'

Farnsworth sat forward with both hands on the desk, fingers spread and palms down as if holding it in place. His face dripped with frustration. 'Nugan-Hand controls some CIA funds. I don't think we need to share that particular information with Martindale, do you?'

'Did Kate Hamilton know?'

With a flat, dead tone, Farnsworth asked, 'What are you getting at, son?'

Palmer sat motionless for a second or two, avoiding Farnsworth's glare. Then he shook his head and said, 'Nothing.'

'All right, then. Go and see Fortescue, have something to eat and be back here at six, sharp.'

Palmer stood, dossier in hand, and left the office.

'What was all that about uranium?' Williams asked.

'Drop it,' came the unambiguous reply. 'Tell me about Palmer. Did he talk to anyone, make any phone calls?'

'You don't trust him?'

'Not with his squeaky-clean background,' Farnsworth replied. 'Did he get in touch with anybody at all?'

'Nope. We've been driving non-stop for three days, so there wasn't—'

'How much did Walker tell you?'

'Who's Walker?'

'You met him in Canberra, didn't you?

'Oh . . . the guy that walked out earlier.'

'Yes.'

'The guy that flew here while we sweated it out in a car for three days?'

'*Yes*, Williams, that guy. Did he tell you about the task force group?'

'He mentioned it. Who is he, anyway?'

Farnsworth grunted and said, 'We asked the Brits to lend a hand with the Whitlam problem and that's what we got. Waltzed in like he owns the fucking place.'

'MI6?'

'No, the surveillance unit in Cheltenham. But he's done a lot of work for Langley in the past, plus he was already in Canberra working undercover in the British Embassy.'

'Doing what?'

'Same as us, trying to find out what the hell Whitlam's up to. It seems the Brits are as frightened of him as we are. Walker's gone along with our plans so far, but he's also got some half-baked idea of getting the Governor-General involved.'

'He didn't look too happy on the way out.'

'That's because I had his house in Canberra bugged. Unfortunately for us, a cypher clerk at the DSD didn't like what he heard and contacted the press.'

'An Aussie clerk?'

'No, one of ours—Tom Stansfield.' Farnsworth drummed his stubby fingers on the desk. 'This could be trouble for us.' He stopped drumming and cracked his neck once more. 'We've secured Stansfield, but he used a music cassette to tape some sensitive traffic and we don't know where it is. It's a plain white cassette with "ND" written on it.'

'ND?'

'Neil Diamond, I'm told.' Farnsworth opened his mouth to continue but sneezed instead. 'Goddamn dust.' Searching his pockets, he pulled out a well-used handkerchief and blew his nose with a long, honking sound. Then he sneezed once more.

'*Gesundheit*,' Williams said.

Farnsworth used a clean corner of the handkerchief to wipe under his eyes. 'There might be enough on that damn tape to hang us all out to dry, not just Walker. I want you to look into it. Start with Stansfield's wife, and report everything back to me. Fortescue has a file ready for you.'

'Okay,' Williams said, leaning forward with his hands braced on the arms of the chair.

'Wait a minute.'

Perched on the edge of the seat, Williams looked uneasy.

'Langley thinks our strategy for getting rid of Whitlam isn't working fast enough,' Farnsworth said. 'So the clowns in Logistics were tasked with finding a solution for us.'

The right side of Williams' face twitched.

'They've decided on a fatal heart attack induced by a poisoned lamington,' Farnsworth continued. 'Apparently, Whitlam's mad keen on lamingtons. Plus he's a big bastard and under a lot of pressure, so I guess they figure a heart attack won't be looked at too closely. They're calling it *Operation Pineapples*.'

'What am I supposed to do, feed them to him?'

'No. If it comes to that, we've got it covered.' Farnsworth rubbed his meaty jaw and said, 'I just want to know . . . what the *hell* is a lamington?'

Williams' upper lip moved—it was a smile of sorts. 'A sponge cake.'

'Is that it?'

'They slice it into small squares, dip the squares in chocolate and roll them in coconut. They're nice. I think the Aussies consider them a national dish.'

'Jesus H. Christ!' Farnsworth snapped. 'We're trying to save these people from themselves and their idea of a culinary delicacy is a fucking sponge cake. Lord help us.'

21. Tragedy

Two days later, Monday 14 July

The brief penned by Palmer provided Martindale with a blueprint of Nugan-Hand's structure and activity. It included detailed records on the bank's founders, Frank Nugan, a law graduate from Sydney University, and Michael J. Hand, a certified American war hero. It also included several faultless reports on the bank's integrity. The Australian and New Zealand Bank reported Nugan-Hand's financial position to be "sound" and its directors "capable and reliable and unlikely to commit the company beyond its means". Hong Kong's Wing-On Bank went even further, guaranteeing with its own money the deposits of Nugan-Hand's elite customers, including the Chase Manhattan Bank and the Fidelity Bank of Philadelphia.

While Martindale was confident that Nugan-Hand was, as he believed, a reputable merchant bank, he was less sure what a search for Merino would reveal.

Armed with the only clue he had—that Merino might be near Alice Springs—Martindale combed the archives of Parliament House for anything he could find on US activity in the Northern Territory. There were four entries. Three related to mining sites far removed from Alice: uranium oxide at Nourlangie Rock, bauxite at Gove Peninsula and manganese at Groote Eylandt. The fourth entry, cross-referenced to the Defence Department, seemed more promising. But all he found was one handwritten note from Prime Minister Harold Holt to his Defence Secretary, stating that an American satellite tracking station was to be constructed twelve miles south-west of Alice Springs.

Alarm bells rang—satellite tracking station sounded rather too much like a political euphemism for missile tracking station. Could he prove it?

Pacing back and forth in his office, fighting the urge to grab a whisky from behind volume ten of Hansard, he remembered something Kate had said to him on their first date: *the local rag is always the best place to get local information*.

*

A short time later, Martindale was sitting alone in the microfiche archive of the National Library searching through back copies of the *Alice Springs Gazette*. He began his search ten years back, one year before Harold Holt's memorandum. A few issues were striking.

Volume Twelve provided confirmation that a US-funded "space research base" was to be built in the Pine Gap valley of the MacDonnell Ranges. The base was expected to take three years to build.

Volume Thirteen displayed several photographs of the Arrernte people being forced off their land, leaving without a struggle, bewildered and unhappy.

Volume Sixteen recorded that a *Joint Defence Space Research Facility* was operational, and that Mr Richard Stallings was Director of Operations.

Volume Twenty recorded that Stallings was forced to retire on the grounds of ill health—Commander James Farnsworth was the new director.

Aside from sporadic reports of misconduct by American servicemen—usually involving booze, a car or a girl, and sometimes all three—Martindale found no further mention of the base.

It was four fifteen. He scoffed a plain cheese sandwich from a vending machine in the library's foyer, and returned to Parliament House for a scheduled meeting with the Prime Minister.

The Prime Minister's Office

With respect covering every inch of his face, Whitlam listened, nodded and sometimes prompted as Martindale revealed Kate's conviction that the CIA had built a secret base close to Alice Springs. Finally, he said, 'Kate was a good reporter, George, but she was wide of the mark on this one. There is an American base not far from Alice, but it has nothing to do with the CIA.'

'She seemed so sure.' Martindale's voice held a strong note of disappointment.

'We have a few CIA operatives working in Australia, but I can't imagine there are any at Alice Springs. If you like, I can get the full register of agents from Arthur Tange in the Defence Department.'

'I'd appreciate that.'

'All right, I will. But rest assured, George, there are no secret bases here.'

'You've never heard of Merino?'

'Only the sheep.'

Remembering his own comment to Kate, the Prime Minister's quip felt like a sharp blow to his gut. 'What does happen at the base near Alice?'

'Research into satellite transmissions,' Whitlam replied. 'Perfect place for it, I'm told.'

'Are we involved?'

'Yes, all information is shared.'

'If it can scan satellite communications,' Martindale said, 'it could also be used to direct missiles.'

'No.' Whitlam shook his head with enough vigour to make the flesh under his chin wobble. 'It's not part of any weapons system, George. No foreign government would ever dream of doing something like that without my knowledge.' He peeked at a diary open on his desk and said, 'I don't suppose you've made any headway in sourcing a loan?'

'A little. I want to start with Steinhart Morgan in Mayfair. It's a medium-sized investment bank, currently pumping heaps of money into Japan.'

'Japan, eh? That could work well for us. The ministry of energy in Japan is looking at new ways to refine uranium, and we have an opportunity of going into partnership with them.' Whitlam raised his brow a notch. 'Who do you know at Steinhart Morgan?'

'No one yet. If the firm pans out, though, I'll bring you a name by the end of the week.'

'Good . . . as long as that name isn't Khemlani.'

Martindale's lips curled upward in a smile, but his eyes remained cold.

One week later

Martindale sat at his desk and, without interest, flicked through that day's edition of *The Canberra Times*. The desk was otherwise quite bare and he looked more than ever unconnected, shrinking up within himself with each page turned.

Thoughts ran through his head like little jolts of electricity: There was no evidence that Nugan-Hand was involved in any illegal activities, or that it had any association with the CIA. Everything in the *Gazette* tallied with the Prime Minister's comments. And Arthur Tange's record of CIA agents working in Australia only had four names on it, none of whom were stationed anywhere near Alice Springs.

He turned a page and took a calming breath. His shoulders slumped and the tension left his arms. Turning another page, a small headline hooked his eye and he scanned the paragraph below it. One name leapt from the print, a name he had come to know only ten days earlier. A feeling of dread overcame him as he read from the start:

Family Tragedy

In the early hours of yesterday morning, Sunday 20 July, a violent explosion ripped through a house on the shores of Lake Monger in suburban Perth. The occupants, Jack and Margaret Donahue, were thought to be sleeping at the time and were found dead in the rubble of the house. The blast was so powerful it levelled the home and blew out the windows of four other houses in the street. "It was a blast like nothing I have ever heard before in my life," said next-door neighbour Matt Davies, who at first thought his own house may have been struck by lightning. "There was total devastation and a strong smell of gas." Forensic examinations by the police and fire services have confirmed that a gas explosion was the cause of the incident. Investigations are ongoing, though the deaths are not thought to be suspicious.

Martindale's heart thumped its beat with the fury of a jackhammer as a thousand scenarios flooded his brain. The office walls folded around him like a prison. Kate's death, he was now certain, was no accident.

Part II

*A*s the weeks passed, a succession of political and intelligence scandals beset Whitlam's government. The Prime Minister reluctantly sacked his friend and colleague, Rex Connor, after the Herald *published documents proving Connor had misled the House about his dealings with Middle Eastern Financier Tirath Khemlani. Connor left a broken man, unable to fathom how his private telexes ended up in the hands of the press. Next to go was Bill Robertson, Head of Australia's overseas intelligence agency, dismissed for assisting CIA activities in Chile and East Timor without Whitlam's approval. Peter Barbour, Head of the domestic agency, was also sacked, ostensibly because of a lengthy overseas business trip he conducted with his secretary. Quietly, however, some speculated that Barbour's dismissal was because the domestic agency was replete with Soviet spies.*

The Opposition parties circled above the corpses, waiting for an excuse to use their power in the Senate to block government funding and force an early election.

The government had yet to secure an overseas loan large enough to neutralise the Opposition's threat.

22. The old man

Sunday 2 November 1975, Canberra

The American Diner across the lake from Parliament House was nothing more than a greasy spoon café to most Canberrans. To Palmer, it was fast food heaven and a welcome slice of downtown California. A family-run business in the comfortable suburb of Reid, its walls were decorated with posters of Hollywood movie stars, its tablecloths were red, white and blue, and its background music was a heady mix of Glenn Miller, Frank Sinatra and Ella Fitzgerald.

Sitting by himself on a bar stool at the far end of the diner's cherry-red counter, Palmer half-heartedly read the breakfast menu—he knew from the moment his alarm clock sounded that he would have pancakes with a side order of bacon and a mug of black coffee.

He looked up as a ringing brass bell over the front door signalled another customer. A rotund man wearing an ill-fitting suit came in and stood for a moment by the door, looking left and right and left again.

Palmer watched as the newcomer ambled past several empty bar stools and sat right next to him, all the while whistling the theme tune from *Hawaii Five-0*. Palmer squirmed in his seat, held the menu closer and buried his nose in it.

The newcomer drummed his fingers on the counter and tapped one foot on the tile floor, both actions in modest synchrony with his whistling. The impromptu display continued for several bars before he suddenly slapped the counter and announced, 'Book 'em, Danno. Murder one.' The accent was hard to pin down, though it certainly wasn't Australian. Or American.

Palmer acknowledged the needless comments with a civil wink.

The stranger returned the same and opened his mouth as if to speak, but instead made a low rasping sound that mutated into a distasteful cough.

Palmer's hands twitched as he repressed the desire to get up and sit somewhere else. He groaned, though not loud enough for anyone to notice, and laid the menu flat.

Covering his mouth with the crook of his elbow, the newcomer coughed twice more. After a brief inspection of his sleeve, he eyed up Palmer and said, 'I will have the waffles. You Americans make good waffles.'

Palmer's toes curled in his shoes.

The newcomer called the waiter over. 'I would like some of your finest tea and a plate of waffles with maple syrup.' With his left arm extended towards Palmer, he said, 'And please bring my friend here a black coffee to go.'

'Excuse me?' Palmer said, his head tilted in bemusement.

'You will not have time for your pancakes and bacon this morning,' the newcomer replied. A sickly smile warped his mouth. 'Another day, perhaps.'

The hairs on Palmer's head bristled. Was this interloper a harmless fanatic of American cop shows who happened to guess what he liked for breakfast, or trouble in fool's clothing?

The waiter hung on, fingering his order pad.

Either way, Palmer thought, eating breakfast sat next to a shoe-tapping, finger-drumming fat lump smelling of pickled fish and hangover would not be pleasant. 'A large black to go, please,' he said to the waiter.

The waiter left.

'Who are you?' Palmer asked.

The entrance bell rang again and the newcomer turned his head. On seeing a young family enter, he looked back at Palmer and said, in singsong fashion, 'I am a friend.'

Before Palmer could respond, the waiter reappeared with a lidded Styrofoam cup. He set the cup down without a word and walked back to the kitchen.

'Okay, friend,' Palmer said. 'Enjoy your waffles.' He stood, left some change on the counter, took the coffee and went to leave.

The newcomer stuck out his arm, blocking Palmer's path.

Palmer's squeeze on the cup caused its lid to pop open. In his mind's eye, he could see himself pouring steaming hot coffee over the full length of the stranger's arm. He straightened his back and, half-consciously flexing his muscles, said, 'If you don't mind?'

'I have a message for you, Mister Palmer.'

Palmer sneered at the use of his name.

'A colleague of mine would like to meet with you.'

'About what?'

'He is waiting for you in the park across the road. You will find him on a bench near the swings.'

'What if I—'

'Goodbye, Mister Palmer.'

*

Palmer stood on the footpath outside the diner, took a swig of coffee and surveyed the gardens and playground opposite. Its colourful shrubs, trimmed grass and shiny swings, all dusted by a solid-blue November sky, did little to dampen the predatory feel it now evoked.

An elderly man, wearing a wide-brimmed hat, business suit and dark glasses, was sitting alone near the children's play area. He appeared to be reading a newspaper. Another man, also suited but considerably younger, was standing in the shadow of a tree at the far end of the park, his head turning from one side to the other. The old man's minder?

Palmer was in no hurry to venture across the road. He sipped his coffee, waiting and watching for anything to happen. Two minutes crawled by but no one entered the grounds—apart from a noisy magpie and stray dog—and the old man and his minder remained in place.

He tossed his near-empty cup into a nearby bin and said, with a pinch of dread creasing his face, 'Let's get this over with.'

Palmer stood a few feet from the bench upon which the old man was sitting, his opener for conversation being nothing more than an upward flick of his head.

The old man folded the newspaper and laid it on his lap. 'Thank you for coming, Mister Palmer.'

Palmer took a step forward. 'Did I have a choice?'

Using both hands, the old man removed his sunglasses. 'Forgive these,' he said, holding the glasses in front of him. 'At my age, you understand, the sun can be very difficult.' He slipped them back on. 'Please take a seat.'

Every fibre of Palmer's being wanted to run, but there was something about the old man that commanded him to stay. His accent was Eastern European, probably Russian. His well-tailored suit was of a style that belonged to a more genteel age. Although he gave the impression of being frail, his voice was strong.

Palmer scanned the trees that dotted the park's perimeter. The old man's minder was now loitering under a different tree, but otherwise he saw nothing untoward.

'You are in no immediate danger, Mister Palmer. Please sit down.'

'No *immediate* danger?'

With a wave of his hand, the old man motioned Palmer to sit.

After one more scan of the park, Palmer did so. 'Who are you and what do you want?' he asked.

The old man reached inside his coat, withdrew his wallet and took out a business card. 'Please,' he said, holding out the card.

Palmer took it and read the embossed print aloud. 'Viktor Dobrogorskiy, Trade Representative, Soviet Embassy, Canberra.'

'I have written my home number on the back,' Dobrogorskiy said. 'You may call me anytime, day or night.'

Palmer flipped it over. A local phone number in copybook handwriting filled the width of the card. 'Why would I want to do that?' he asked.

'You do understand, do you not, that I have very little knowledge about international trade?'

'Yes, I understand.' Palmer fidgeted with the business card, bending it up and down between his hands. 'What I don't—'

'Tell me,' Dobrogorskiy interrupted, 'did you ever meet Katherine Hamilton?'

Palmer turned his head and stared at his reflection in the old man's sunglasses. 'Why do you ask that?'

'I met her once at an embassy function. They are mostly tiresome affairs, but that night was different. Miss Hamilton was a

112

delight to be with, even for an old man like myself. She had a sharp mind and the most beautiful, expressive eyes I have ever seen.'

'She's dead,' Palmer said flatly.

'Yes . . . it is a great shame. Professor Martindale's female companions have a tendency to die before their time.' He paused. 'How familiar are you with the good professor?'

Palmer shook his head, trying to make sense of what he was hearing. A dozen questions leapt through his mind, but he didn't voice any of them.

Sliding the newspaper close to Palmer, Dobrogorskiy asked, 'Are you aware that unfortunate deaths follow Professor Martindale wherever he goes?' He tapped the paper. 'This is a few months old, but I thought you might like to read the article on page seventeen about Miss Hamilton's mother.'

Palmer looked at the paper but didn't take it. 'I would appreciate you getting to the point because . . . .'

Dobrogorskiy turned his head in the direction of the diner.

Palmer did the same. Only then did he notice that the malodourous stranger from the diner was now lurking by its entrance, smoking a cigarette.

'The point is, Mister Palmer, we would like you to work for us.'

With the look of a child lost in a crowded arcade, Palmer gave a slow, unconvincing headshake. 'There is nothing you could do or say to make me want to do that.'

Dobrogorskiy replied, in a tone of voice that was both fatherly and respectful, 'You may be right. We recognize you are loyal to your country. That is precisely the reason why we have approached you and no one else. We are aware of your record at the training academy. And we are also aware you have serious concerns about your assignment here in Australia.'

'How could you possibly know that?

The question was ignored as the old man continued, 'The simple fact is, Mister Palmer, you do not understand what you are involved in. The deaths that follow Professor Martindale are not accidents.'

Palmer peered at the newspaper that lay between them. 'Martindale wasn't mixed up with Kate Hamilton's death. I know for a fact he was doing everything he could to find out what happened to her.'

'I think it is more likely Professor Martindale was doing everything he could to protect himself.'

'Protect himself from what?'

Dobrogorskiy raised his hands, palms open, and gave the slightest shrug. 'You tell me.'

Palmer twisted to face the old man head-on. 'If you have something to say, say it.' Quelling the shrill in his voice, he added, 'Otherwise, I'm gone.'

'Very well, I will explain all that I can.' Dobrogorskiy's manner was businesslike. 'What we want is for Mister Whitlam to remain in office. He has signed agreements to allow full scientific and technical cooperation between Russia and Australia, and we want to honour those agreements. In time, we expect new commercial and cultural exchanges to take place between our countries.' He shook his head before adding, 'American interference is destroying these opportunities, not only for us but also for Australia. Unlike America, we are not pretending to be Australia's friend. The Prime Minister is a good man and we do not wish to see him assassinated.'

'I know full well why the Soviet Union wants Whitlam to stay in power, and it doesn't have anything to do with scientific or business agreements. And while we might prefer Whitlam gone . . . .' He gave a short, puzzled laugh. 'You're crazy if you think we would assassinate him.'

The old man gave back a broad smile, his rounded cheeks pushing against the frame of his glasses. 'You are wrong on both counts. You have been played like a puppet, and soon your masters may well cut the strings.'

'I don't believe a word you're saying.' Palmer's voice was weak; his words trailed off.

'You consider we want Mister Whitlam to remain in office because he might put an end to Merino. Is that not so?'

Palmer snatched a breath.

'Yes, young man, we are familiar with Merino. Should the Prime Minister choose to remove it, the CIA would simply build another unit somewhere else. All it would cost them is money, which should not present any great hardship for them. Please examine the Nugan-Hand Bank a little more closely. See for yourself how much money your paymasters have, and what they are doing with it.'

Palmer, his lips dry, had no answer to the old man's words.

'So you see,' Dobrogorskiy went on, 'it does not matter to us what happens to Merino.' His mouth curled a little and he coughed once. 'I have fought injustice all my life. Sometimes, I have to admit, the morality of the fight was questionable. Though not in this instance. What is happening to Mister Whitlam is—'

'Stop! Please don't tell me you're doing this for the benefit of Whitlam. I'm not so gullible to believe the KGB would put Australia's interests ahead of its own. If this is not about Merino, then what is it about?'

Dobrogorskiy stared into the distance and took a long time to answer. When he did talk, there was a streak of sadness in his voice.

'I expect it comes down to what my work has always been about—money and power. Only this time there is more at issue than usual.'

Palmer knew the old man was choosing his words with caution. His breath came in shallow bursts as he hung on every syllable.

'You could help us a great deal, Mister Palmer.'

'Help how? You haven't told me anything yet.'

Dobrogorskiy looked over to the young man standing under the tree and gave him some kind of hand signal. To Palmer, he said, 'It is not safe for us to stay here any longer.' He took hold of the newspaper and stood.

Palmer stood also.

'Katherine Hamilton did not deserve to die,' Dobrogorskiy said. 'Neither did her mother.' He offered the paper to Palmer.

This time, Palmer took it.

'And they will not be the last to die in this affair,' Dobrogorskiy continued. 'You may not believe this, young man, but I do not wish the same fate for you.'

The old man's minder and the stranger from the café were approaching fast.

'You know where to contact me, Mister Palmer. For your own benefit, I hope you will do so soon.' Dobrogorskiy tipped his hat and left.

23. The dead drop

Later that Sunday

Martindale was settled at his desk with a mug of hot coffee when the intercom buzzed. He flipped the switch for Mrs Henderson and said, 'I see I'm not the only one working on a Sunday.'

'Indeed, George. Your boss left me plenty to do for the finance summit. I will likely be here till midnight.'

'Sorry 'bout that.'

'Never mind. I'm calling because Security are holding a young woman in King's Hall by the name of Cathy Stansfield. Is she a friend of yours?'

'No.'

'She insists on seeing you.'

'About what?'

'She won't say. Apparently, she's very upset . . . and *very* pregnant.'

He managed the beginning of a smile. 'Well, it isn't mine.'

'I'm sure not. But they're worried she will have the baby right there in the hall if you don't meet with her.'

'Couldn't you sort this out for me, June?'

'Sorry. Mister Hayden needs me.'

'Is *everybody* in today?'

'I have to go, George.'

'All right,' he said, 'ask Security to bring her 'round.'

'Very well.'

'She doesn't have a gun or anything, does she?'

'Let's hope not, George.'

*

Martindale's unease evaporated the moment he saw the young woman's soulful eyes and distended belly. He asked her to take a seat beside his desk. As she squeezed by him in the doorway, he could see her cheeks were wet from crying and her nose was runny; a vague scent of cheap perfume trailed her. He told the guard to wait in the anteroom, left the door open and sat back at his desk. 'Have we met before, Missus Stansfield?'

With her face tilted down, she sniffed once and shook her head.

'How did you know I would be here today . . . on a Sunday, I mean?'

She looked up. The light on her face wasn't kind: the tip of her nose was bright red, and she had blotchy skin and a rash of tiny pimples across her forehead. 'I didn't realize it was Sunday,' she replied.

Her American twang, as much as her answer, took Martindale by surprise. 'How can I help you?' he asked.

'It's about my husband, Tom Stansfield. Do you know him?'

'I don't think so.'

Her eyes widened a little and she held his gaze for a long moment before stating, 'He was working here in Canberra for the Defence Signals Directorate, on secondment from the CIA.' A tear

118

traced the path of a previous tear down her right cheek. She wiped it away with the back of her hand.

'Would you like a drink, Missus Stansfield?'

She shook her head. 'Tom was arrested four months ago for treason.' Her tears kept coming.

'I'm sorry to hear that, but why have you come to see me?'

'Katherine Hamilton!' The name was spat out as though it was a curse. 'She was your girlfriend, wasn't she?'

Without a trace of sympathy in his voice, he said, 'Tell me why you're here.'

'Tom was passing information to her.'

Martindale glanced at the open door before asking, in a quiet voice, 'What sort of information?'

'Classified stuff, I guess. They arrested Tom on the same night Miss Hamilton died, and then sent him back to the States to stand trial for treason. And yesterday—'

'Wait a minute,' Martindale said, holding up a hand. He stood, walked over to the door, dismissed the guard, closed the door and took his seat again. 'Go on.'

'Yesterday, I found out that Tom was given a life sentence with a non-parole period of forty years. Forty years!' she repeated.

He grimaced. 'Maybe you should start from the beginning. Exactly *who* arrested your husband?'

'The CIA I think, but who knows with these people? They were all American, except for the man in charge. He was English, I'm sure.'

'Did you get his name?'

'No.'

'What did he look like?'

She shrugged. 'Ordinary . . . apart from his eyebrows. His hair was white but he had these thick, black eyebrows.'

119

Martindale shifted in his chair. Below the desk, out of sight, his right fist clenched tight. 'Tell me about Miss Hamilton. How do you know she was involved?'

'She phoned our home once, but hung up as soon as I answered. I thought Tom might have been having an affair, so I made him tell me who it was. He said Miss Hamilton was doing a documentary on the security services and that he was her liaison officer.' Nursing her unborn child with both arms, she went on, 'I wanted to believe him but . . . .'

'Kate was investigating the CIA,' Martindale said.

'Then she must have found something they didn't want her to find.'

'Meaning?'

'Meaning, that's why she's dead. Tom tried to call her the night she died but no one answered the phone.'

Because, Martindale thought, Kate was in my apartment.

'Tom said she might be in danger. He grabbed his bowling bag and—'

'He went bowling?'

Her tightly screwed lips told him to shut up and listen.

'Tom was using a locker at the bowling alley to pass information to her.'

'A dead-drop,' Martindale offered.

'What?'

'Doesn't matter.'

'He got back about an hour later, empty-handed and scared as hell. Almost as soon as he walked in, they forced our door open and arrested him. Then they tore our house apart looking for some secret tape recording Tom made. That was four months ago and I haven't seen him since.'

The intercom buzzed.

Martindale ignored it. 'Why wait until now to come and see me?'

'They've been watching me like a hawk. I knew if I did anything suspicious, I might never see Tom again. But after yesterday, I had to do something.'

There were two knocks on the door. It opened and Mrs Henderson stepped one pace into the room.

The young woman did not turn around.

Martindale's silent glare signalled his wish for Mrs Henderson to leave.

'Just checking if you need anything,' Mrs Henderson said with her eyes fixed on the back of the young woman's head.

'We're fine, June.'

'The guard didn't stay?'

'I dismissed him. I'll call you in a few minutes.'

Mrs Henderson responded with a polite smile and left, closing the door behind her.

'My husband's a good man, Mister Martindale, and he wouldn't have betrayed his country for nothing. I went to the bowling alley this morning hoping to find the tape, thinking there might be something on it to help Tom's case. But there was no locker in his name.' She paused, tilting her head a little. 'Do you think the locker could be in Miss Hamilton's name?'

'Possibly.'

'If it is in her name, they might open it for you.'

'I doubt that,' Martindale answered.

'But with your position, couldn't you get a search warrant or something?

Without any conviction in his voice, he said, 'I'll see what I can do.' It sounded pathetic, even to him.

The last vestige of faith in her eyes vanished; her lower lip trembled. 'All I want is to have Tom back.'

Out of pity, Martindale said, 'I could speak with the American Ambassador, but I can't promise anything. I'll try to . . . .' Something flickered in his eyes. 'Tell me . . . which bowling centre was it?'

'Southern Cross.'

He took hold of a pen. 'What's your phone number?'

She gave it.

'I might be able to help, Missus Stanfield, but I need to check something first. Go home now and I'll call you as soon as I can.'

*

With no traffic, Martindale reached his apartment in under twelve minutes. He walked straight through to the laundry, opened the ironing board cupboard and removed a small screwdriver pegged to the inside of the door. He then went back through the apartment to the master bedroom's *en suite* and unscrewed the bath panel. A cardboard tube, eighteen inches long and coated in a fine layer of dust, lay behind the drainage pipe. He grabbed the tube, tapped it on the floor to dislodge some dust, walked through to the kitchen and laid it on the table.

He took a beer from the fridge, sat at the table and gulped most of it. Another swig and it was empty. Eyeing the tube, he said, 'What are you waiting for?' He picked it up, popped the lid off, pinched the sheet of rolled paper within and pulled it out. With more care than was needed, he smoothed the roll flat and used the palms of his outstretched hands to keep it from springing back.

The familiar stroke of Kate's hand hit him raw at every turn of his eye—a snapshot of her friends, her work and her play. As he hoped, *Southern Cross Bowling* was scribbled smack in the middle of the roll. He remembered seeing the name before and thinking how alien it appeared in her otherwise unsporting life. This time, he also saw the reference to locker number twenty-four and the nearby sequence of numbers. What other details had he missed? His eyes danced over the words, settling mostly on her unconscious hand—small hearts scattered above his name, little stick-birds flying between the detail, swirls and curls. He leant forward and kissed her memory.

Stephen J Anderson

24. Six rounds

Reginald Xavier Walker was born and raised in London and
educated at Balliol College, Oxford, where he took a double
first in classics and law. After a short stint at the Foreign Office,
he transferred to the Government Communications Headquarters
(GCHQ) in Cheltenham. Within five years, his rank was Chief
Liaison Officer to America's National Security Agency, where his
assignments often included visits to the CIA in Langley. At
Langley, he quickly became known for finding unique solutions to
challenging problems, solutions that were sometimes legal and
sometimes not.

On the far side of middle age and of average height, weight and
build, Walker's only distinguishing characteristic—set against a
head of white hair—was his bushy, black eyebrows. Speculation
about his private life varied from happily married through to
devout homosexual—no one was sure. He moved to Canberra a
year after Whitlam came to power, spending most of his time at
Yarra Lodge, a mock-Edwardian manor house on the western edge
of the city. Yarra was the gift of the British taxpayer and came
complete with a pool, gardener and part-time domestic help.
GCHQ listed the entire expense as overseas business, hospitality
and travel.

Walker's day usually ended with a tall glass of Pimm's and a meat dish of some sort, which he ate alone in front of the six o'clock news. Jenny, the nineteen-year-old housemaid, prepared the meal for him. If there was a Mrs Walker, Jenny never saw her.

Early evening, that same day

Pimm's in hand, Walker switched on the television in the corner of the lounge and turned the channel selector to nine. The screen flickered into life with the pre-news adverts still playing. With his free hand, he wriggled the rabbit ears of the indoor aerial to sharpen the picture.

Jenny slipped in, flushed-faced, with a plate of roast chicken and a wooden smile.

Walker cocked his head to look at her. 'Ah, good.'

She placed the chicken on a side table between two armchairs.

From afar, he eyed the offering. 'Where's the gravy?'

'It's coming,' she said while making a beeline for the exit.

He called after her. 'I could hear your music earlier.'

She stopped just short of the door and turned.

'Elton John, if I'm not mistaken.' His nostrils flared. 'Must you play it so loud?'

'Sorry.' Her look said otherwise.

Jenny left and Walker went back to fiddling with the rabbit ears.

Good evening Australia. This is Brian Henderson with the National Nine News at six o'clock. In the news tonight: political disaster for the Opposition leaders as Prime Minister Whitlam accuses the CIA of funding the National Country Party. Also in the news...

His hand recoiled from the aerial.

...Italian film director, Pier Pasolini, murdered by a seventeen-year-old boy, and Prince Carlos of Spain takes over as provisional Head of State after General Franco steps down.

Jenny re-entered the lounge. 'Here's your gravy.'

Walker kept watching the TV.

She put two fingers up to him, placed the gravy boat next to the chicken and left.

He stepped backwards and sat on the edge of one armchair. Clasping his Pimm's with both hands, he spun it round and round.

Following his press conference in Alice Springs yesterday, Prime Minister Whitlam helped celebrate the Diamond Jubilee at the Diocese of Willochra. In eighty-four degree heat, a four-hundred strong crowd of staunch Labor supporters had gathered on Miller's football field on the outskirts of town to hear one of the Prime Minister's now-familiar defiant speeches. He began reading from a prepared speech, outlining the House of Representative's right to govern without obstruction by the Senate. The Prime Minister argued that, by refusing to pass the money bills, the Senate is in effect blackmailing the government. Malcolm Fraser and Doug Anthony, he added, are deliberately holding the country to ransom. Then, departing from his written notes, Whitlam faced the crowd and dropped a bombshell, openly accusing the Opposition of receiving support from the CIA.

Walker watched, open-mouthed, as the familiar figure of Gough Whitlam filled the screen.

We must get on with the budget; we must get on with the economic recovery; we must get people back to work. And we must make it plain to the Australian people who are the guilty men. Every weekend Fraser and Anthony get more and more desperate in their abuse of me. But I've had no associations with CIA money in Australia, as Anthony has…

'Jesus Christ in heaven!' Walker said.

…My wife hasn't received any sixteen thousand dollar necklaces for launching ships overseas, as Sinclair's wife did. I haven't got, or my family hasn't got, superphosphate subsidies, as Fraser's has. No income tax troubles in my family. That is, they've been able to get nothing on me. And they're getting more and more desperate, these men who are subsidised by the CIA or overseas shipbuilders, or the superphosphate people. They're getting more and more desperate in their personal abuse of me and the whole of the Labor government.

Brian Henderson reappeared.

Within minutes of Mister Whitlam's speech, the media in Canberra descended on Doug Anthony, who commented the Prime Minister must be losing his grip when he resorts to such fabrications. Anthony denied any involvement with the CIA and said that suggestions to the contrary were simply ludicrous. He would not comment further except to say he would be making a statement in Parliament tomorrow, and that following his statement he would be expecting a full and frank apology from Prime Minister Whitlam.

A whiff of roast chicken broke Walker's stupor. He swallowed hard.

Mister Whitlam's revelation of possible CIA intrusion into Australian politics was quick to reach Washington. Just before coming to air, our Washington correspondent, Jim Marshall, caught up with US Secretary of State, Doctor Henry Kissinger…

Walker's body curled forward as though a river of dread was flowing over him.

... as he arrived at Harvard University to attend a fundraising event. Marshall reported that Doctor Kissinger dismissed the Prime Minister's comments as fanciful. Doctor Kissinger added that such a false charge against the Country Party leader could have damaging effects on other aspects of Australian-US relations.

'You pretentious, egotistical clown,' Walker trumpeted. 'For once, couldn't you keep your mouth shut?'

After the break: Italian film director run over and killed by a seventeen-year-old boy.

As the National Nine jingle blared, Walker set his drink down, strode across to the television and struck the off button. He then walked out of the lounge and into the central hallway of the house. Muffled sounds of Elton John were everywhere and he flashed his eyes at the kitchen door. 'Bloody girl,' he said as he crossed the hall into the room opposite.

The downstairs study was dominated by a hefty oak desk that sat alone near the centre of the room, and a dozen or so of Walker's finished and unfinished watercolours of the Australian bush. Behind the desk stood a drinks cabinet—stocked to the brim with six varieties of Pimm's—and an iron-grey, freestanding safe. Walker headed for the safe.

Bent on one knee, he turned the combination lock back and forth, spun the five-pronged handle anticlockwise and opened the safe. It contained several neat stacks of fifty-dollar bills and one stack of brown manila folders. A box of Smith and Wesson cartridges and a small address book were lying on top of the folders. He took hold of the address book and flipped through its pages, stopping at the letter F.

Seated at his desk, Walker picked up the phone and clipped a scrambling unit over the mouthpiece and a decoder over the earpiece. He dialled an out-of-area number. Once answered, he activated the scrambler and waited for the telltale hum of a secure connection before asking, 'Did you see the news?'

Listening to the reply, Walker's face turned a deep shade of red. He held the phone away and eyed it as though it was a lump of excrement. Bringing it close again, he said, 'This is *precisely* what I feared, Farnsworth. If you carry through with that operation, you'll destroy everything I have worked for.'

Walker's hold on the phone tightened. 'If Whitlam happens to drop dead only weeks before Merino's lease is due to be renewed, you won't have to fret about your precious little spy hut anymore because the whole bloody CIA will disappear. The American Senate has had enough of your dirty little schemes and, frankly, so has the rest of the world. In case you still don't get it, let me tell you that the days of the CIA being able to knock off anyone they choose are over.' There was no reply, so Walker persisted. 'The loans fiasco has worked well for us so far, and it gives the Governor-General legal justification to take action against Whitlam. I have spent months priming Kerr to do precisely that. And in a day or two, the Chief Justice himself will brief Kerr on his rightful obligations. As soon as that happens, Kerr *will* dismiss Whitlam.' Walker added, almost to himself, 'Especially as Charteris said he won't lose his job as Governor-General.'

Listening, Walker lifted his eyes to the ceiling. 'Sir Martin Charteris is the Queen's Private Secretary,' he said. '*That* should tell you a lot. If you don't interfere and let everything progress as planned, we could all be home for Christmas.'

He cut off Farnsworth's manic rambling with, 'There is one more thing you should be crystal-clear about. *Never* threaten me again. Now, goodbye.' He detached the scrambler and decoder, discarded them on the desk and hung up the phone.

Walker moved across to the drinks cabinet. Perched on it was the only luxury item he brought with him from England—a large dark blue whisky decanter. He pulled out the ornate glass stopper and poured a double shot. With the stopper back in place, he raised the decanter, rotating it slightly, and withdrew the small-calibre, snub-nosed revolver wedged in its thickset base. He set the decanter down and inspected the gun's chamber. Six rounds. Satisfied, he replaced the gun, grabbed his whisky and walked to the kitchen.

He called for Jenny.

She was gone.

25. A simple plan

Martindale stood from the kitchen table and stepped over to the open window. In the field opposite, under a sunset sky of burnt orange, four teenage boys were in the final throes of their cricket game. He watched as the batsman sent the ball flying into a eucalyptus. Shouts of "six" were smothered by a horde of squawking crows escaping the feral ball. The boys ducked in unison as a few crazed birds swooped low over their heads. The batsman took a swipe at one of them, missed and fell to the ground. They all laughed. One minute later—ball, stumps and scattered drink cans in hand—they left. The field was empty. The street was empty. The squawking continued.

He turned and let his weight fall against the windowsill. The sheet of paper ripped from Kate's desk pad lay on the kitchen table, held in place with a whiskey bottle at one end and a fruit bowl at the other. He went back to the table and smoothed the paper flat, his eyes remaining rooted to the scribbled details of *Southern Cross Bowling*. As the last rays of sunlight skimmed the paper's surface, he took a moment to calm his heart, steady his thoughts and hatch a plan. Then he walked through to the bedroom to get ready.

His plan was simple: dressed for the part in blue jeans, sweatshirt and tennis shoes, he would drive to the bowling alley, raid the contents of locker number twenty-four and return home. To lessen the chance of being recognised, Martindale swapped his contacts for an old pair of spectacles with big teardrop frames and lightly tinted lenses. His vision was a little patchy, but it was good enough.

It was gone eight o'clock when he walked back to the kitchen and took a last look out the window. The trees in the field stood as shadows against the mist of city lights. The hum of distant traffic had dissolved, and the crows were silent.

*

Martindale drove half a mile east to where the city ended and suburbia began. It was the land of redbrick houses and the Holden Kingswood. Dim streetlights completed the picture of ordinary.

Turning left into Flinders Way, he spotted a lone Mercedes travelling a few lengths behind. Four hundred yards on, he turned right into Wattle Road and then right again into Ginninderra. The Mercedes did the same.

At the first intersection, he made a rapid U-turn. The red taillights of the Mercedes grew faint in his rear-view mirror, finally disappearing. Cheeks puffed with a hesitant smile, he relaxed his squeeze on the steering wheel, made another U-turn and sped on to the sports centre.

Manicured grass verges gave way to tarmac; dull street lamps gave way to brilliant neon. He went past the car park entrance, turned left at the next crossroad and pulled to the kerb outside one of Canberra's standard-issue bungalows. There was no Mercedes in the rear-view, no vehicles of any description. His brow unknotted and he breathed easy.

Martindale switched the engine off and, for a minute or two, was transfixed by the display of domesticity that surrounded him: a kitchen light off here, a bedroom light on there. He knew every house on the street, every house on the block. They were all the same: three bedrooms, one bathroom, a front yard brimming with ornamental shrubs and a backyard crowded with toys, bikes and the occasional aboveground pool. He knew because suburban comfort had been *his* reality, man and boy.

After checking the road behind was still empty, he left on foot for the bowling alley.

*

Stood in front of locker number twenty-four, Martindale looked around. It was half an hour before closing time but already two men were walking the far lanes with wide, soft brooms. A third was emptying bins. Although the bar still buzzed with customers, drinking or playing pinball, no one was bowling.

He keyed in what he hoped was the correct code and turned the handle through ninety degrees. The locker opened. Inside was a canvas bag with a striped beach towel draped over it. Martindale pushed the towel aside, pulled the bag forward and unzipped it. A sizeable bed of cash and the barrel of a silver handgun stared back at him. Without any noticeable change of expression, he took the bag and closed the locker.

*

In the protective shadows at the car park's edge, Martindale knelt on one knee to examine the bag's contents. Nudging the pistol to one side, he dug a path through the money and moved his hand along the base. His fingers met two hard-backed envelopes and he dragged them free. One envelope contained three unstamped passports—Australian, New Zealand and American, all in the name of Tom Stansfield. The other had a thin ledger detailing money transfers from Nugan-Hand to the Cayman Islands, plus half a dozen papers—all marked top secret—on uranium mining.

With his eyes fixed on the pistol's trigger, he furrowed through the money again. This time his fingers struck the hard edge of a small cassette. Was it Mrs Stanfield's missing tape? He put the cassette into his back pocket, checked to see if the pistol was loaded—it was—and tucked it down the front of his jeans. With the bag in hand, he walked on.

Try as he might, Martindale's car key would not slide into the door lock. Stooping for a closer look, a gentle smile took hold when he saw that someone had forced a matchstick into the lock— it had been a favourite pastime of his boyhood gang to stuff matches into the locks of expensive foreign motorcars, which in his neighbourhood was anything other than a Ford or Holden. With a certain sense of pride that his modest Corolla received such treatment, he pinched the tip of the match and wriggled it free. The shuffle of feet behind barely registered before he felt a stinging blow to the back of his head. His knees buckled. He reached out to stop himself from falling, when another blow hurled him face-first into the car door.

26. Windfall

Williams took a long, steady look at the surrounding area. The only sign of life was the flicker of television sets from a few curtained living rooms on both sides of the street. He tightened his grip on the bloodied iron rod and brought it down once more on Martindale's head, this time with the might of a guillotine's crush of flesh and bone. He then plucked the canvas bag from the gutter and headed for his Mercedes, parked in the darkness beyond.

Obeying every traffic law he knew or imagined, Williams drove north-west towards the inner suburb of Lyneham. A mile on, he stopped beside a vacant lot. With the engine running, he hit the interior roof light, unzipped the bag and looked inside. The corners of his mouth turned up, rising until his cheeks resembled pink golf balls.

Twenty minutes later, Williams parked on the drive of a nondescript two-up two-down boarding house at the end of a cul-de-sac. Hugging the sports bag under one arm, he entered the house, deadlocked the door and went up the narrow staircase to the front bedroom. Lit only by a shaft of light from the street lamp, he crossed to the window and scanned the immediate neighbourhood. He saw nothing unusual; the only sound he heard was next door's yapping Chihuahua.

With the curtains drawn and the ceiling light on, Williams upturned the bag over the bed. Three passports, a small money ledger and a torrent of inch thick bundles of cash rained down. He plucked a bundle from the pile and flicked through it—they were all fifties. He did the same with another bundle. And another. Leaning forward, he put his snout to the cash and took a deep breath.

At that moment, the doorbell rang. Williams quickly gathered the passports and ledger, levelled the mound of notes with a sweep of his arm, threw a blanket over them and walked downstairs.

Farnsworth looked around the sitting room at the bare walls and tired furniture, his face wrinkled at the stench leaping from the shag-pile carpet. 'What do you think of our new safe house?'

Williams gave a modest twitch of his face.

Niceties completed, Farnsworth asked, 'Where's Palmer?'

'He didn't show.'

Farnsworth's mouth tightened and stretched as if he'd swallowed a glass of undiluted lemon juice. 'Please tell me you found the tape.'

Williams held out the passports and ledger. That's everything Martindale had on him. All the passports are in Tom Stansfield's name.'

'No tape?'

'Nope.'

'*Jeeesus*.' Farnsworth skimmed through the money ledger, squinting hard at a couple of pages. 'What the hell did Stansfield expect to achieve with this?'

Williams shrugged.

'I take it, at least, that Martindale's off our hands?'

'Yes.'

'Witnesses?'

'None.'

'Good.' Farnsworth held the ledger out and said, with a more composed voice, 'Stansfield couldn't run with just this as insurance. Maybe that young wife of his gave Martindale the tape when she saw him at Parliament House.'

'Maybe there is no tape,' Williams offered.

'Trust me, there is. And Stansfield must have had a load of money stacked away as well. You can't run without money.'

The Adam's apple in Williams' throat moved up and down.

'We're done for if that tape ever surfaces,' Farnsworth went on. 'Check Martindale's apartment again. Tear it apart if you have to. And when you're finished with that, find Palmer.'

'And do what with him?'

'After Whitlam's gone, we'll need to tie up all loose ends. That might mean taking care of Palmer as well.'

'I thought the kid didn't know anything.'

'I'm not taking any chances,' Farnsworth replied. 'Palmer's name was mentioned twice over the past week in calls made from the Russian embassy. I think someone there is trying to turn him . . . or they *have* turned him.'

'If Martindale and the kid both die in the same—'

'I don't want you to kill him—not right away, at least. Just bring him to me. Pretend everything's normal and we might catch him out with the Russians.' Farnsworth's face distorted into a sneer. 'Then we can arrange for him to be bunking with Stansfield for the next forty years.'

'You want him at Merino?' Williams asked with dread.

'No. I'm staying at Hotel Canberra until this job's finished, room twelve. '

Williams looked down at a large carpet stain creeping out from under a threadbare chair and said, under his breath, 'Okay for some.'

27. The tape

Police vans littered the entire area, choking the soupy night air with their flashing blue lights. Down near the water's edge, powerful searchlights chased something in the lake. A throng of people had gathered on the bridge above, peering down over the railings. On the ground, uniformed officers kept onlookers at bay. Everywhere, the stench of diesel and human stink.

His hands were bloody; he was soaking wet.

And Sarah was gone.

'Sarah,' Martindale called.

His eyelids crept open. Anchored to the ground with his left ear and shoulder set hard against the car door, all he saw was a blurred image of his keys lying on the road. He blinked a few times expecting the image to clear. Nothing changed.

'Are you all right, mate?' came a male voice.

The voice was not strong enough to puncture the high-pitched ringing that clogged Martindale's head.

'Are you all right?'

This time Martindale heard the voice, though not the question. Twisting to face the visitor, the back of his head exploded in pain. 'Oh, Jesus!'

Placing a hand on Martindale's shoulder, the visitor said, 'You need a doctor, mate. Your head's bleeding.'

Martindale sat upright against the car, his face alive with agony, and felt three sticky-wet lumps at the back of his head, one the size of an egg.

'What happened to you?' the visitor asked.

'I can't see properly.'

'One of your lenses is smashed.' The visitor looked Martindale over. 'Have you come from the bowling club?'

Martindale took a sudden, short intake of breath. 'Where's the bag?'

'What bag?'

'I had a sports bag. It was right here.'

'There wasn't any bag when I got here.'

Martindale squinted at the visitor. 'Who are you?'

'Who am *I*? I live here, mate. Who are *you*?'

Martindale ignored him and reached for his back pocket. As he did, the front of his jersey drifted up, exposing the gun.

The visitor moved back one pace.

Martindale pulled out the cassette.

'Maybe I should call the cops,' the visitor said.

'I tripped, that's all,' Martindale replied. He held the cassette to his chest.

'Whatever you say, mate.'

Martindale gripped his keys and, braced against the car, slid to his feet. 'You don't need to worry,' he said to the visitor, 'I won't be coming back.'

*

The drive home wasn't easy. The left lens of Martindale's spectacles formed a mosaic of images across his retina, and the lumps on his skull asserted their presence every few seconds. After running a red light at a pedestrian crossing, he stopped and poked his thumb through the shattered lens, scattering small chunks of glass over his thighs and the seat of the car. He carried on home with as much diligence as he could muster with one good eye and a rhythmic pounding in his head.

Martindale pulled onto his driveway and came to an abrupt stop. Looking up at his apartment, he saw a faint green light drift from the lounge to the kitchen. A shadow emerged at the window. 'Bastards,' he said under his breath. He immediately backed away and drove to downtown Canberra. At Coronation Avenue, he turned right for Parliament House.

Parked in his usual spot, Martindale went to the rear of the car, gave a hurried glance over his shoulder and opened the boot. Its light was dim and flickered. He removed the pistol from his trousers, tucked it into the well of the spare tyre and concealed it with his sailing jacket and an assortment of fishing paraphernalia. He then slammed the boot down and walked into the House.

The bronze statue of George V cut a lonely figure in Kings Hall. No reporters. No lobbyists. No ministers seeking a shot of glory on the late night news. Only a security guard was present, seated with the Sunday sports pages spread out before him.

To hide the folly of his suburban adventure and ease passage past the guard, Martindale removed his mangled specs and covered the back of his head by pretending to scratch it. The foyer was a blur but he knew it well enough to navigate his way to the West Block.

'There aren't any tennis courts in here, Professor,' the guard said as Martindale walked by.

Martindale stopped and looked in the guard's general direction. He couldn't recognise the face and didn't know the voice. 'Sorry, what?'

'The tennis shoes?'

'Oh . . . while the boss is away, eh?'

The guard went back to his newspaper.

Once in the corridor of the West Block, Martindale slipped into the men's toilet to check his wounds. The lumps on his head were as big as ever and the throbbing lingered on. Mercifully, the bleeding had stopped. Holding his breath, he coerced a mattered clump of hair into hiding the damage. He then cupped a handful of water from the basin tap, splashed his face and wiped it dry. Knowing he had a spare set of contact lenses in his office, he tossed his spectacles into the bin and left.

The final barrier to his own sanctuary was Mrs Henderson. She was, as promised, still in her office preparing for the finance summit. He passed her office in silence.

*

At first, all he heard was the persistent hiss of a poor quality tape. Then came the muted sounds of a chattering mob, pierced twice by a woman laughing. Next, a lone violin cut through the chatter with three simple notes. A second violin merged, followed by the towering voice of a full orchestra.

Martindale only needed the first note from the first violin to identify what the letters "ND" on the cassette stood for. Hopeful the damage to his skull had reaped more than a pirated copy of Neil

Diamond's *Hot August Night*, he fast-forwarded two minutes—
Crunchy Granola Suite was in full swing. He left the tape playing
and let his body sink into the chair.

There was a knock on the door; his body jerked up and he
stopped the tape.

The door swung open.

'Hello, June.' It was not a warm welcome.

'Sorry to interrupt. I noticed you walk by, and thought I'd check
to see if you needed anything before I go home.'

'Nothing, thanks. I'll be going myself in a few minutes.'

'That's probably just as well, George. You look terrible.'

He eyed the tape.

Mrs Henderson did the same and took a small step into the room.
'Was that Neil Diamond you were playing?'

His head went back a little. 'I didn't know you were a fan.'

'I'm not, but my neighbour plays that album constantly.'

He affected a brief smile.

'I'll leave you to it, George.' She left, closing the door behind
her.

Martindale waited sufficient time for Mrs Henderson to exit his
anteroom, and then pressed the play button. Moments later the
music ended and a hissing noise returned. A few sharp crackles
came next. Then . . .

Where the fuck were you?

His whole body shuddered at the sound of Kate's voice.

I was there.

Bullshit, Fred. I was bang on time, so don't—

Calm down, Kate! He turned up a few minutes early,
worried sick someone was following him.

Shit.

143

I tried to get him to wait for you but he wasn't having any of it. Either I went with him there and then or it was all over.

Did he bring the proof?

No.

Oh, fuck! I can't—

He'll get the proof we need.

When?

A few days, he said.

A few days! Christ, Fred, how much longer is he going to string us along? Is he for real?

He is, I'm sure of it.

Freddie, if we're wrong about Cairns—

We're not wrong. He said the loans letter was a definite fake, and your hunch about Merino is spot on. It is the American base near Alice and they're using it to spy on everyone.

Shit.

They've been undermining Whitlam for months. And get this, Kate . . . the Governor-General's involved.

Kerr? Involved how?

Don't know, but somehow Kerr is part of the plan to get rid of Whitlam.

This is crazy. I've got to tell George.

No!

He could help us, Fred.

Don't, Kate. I wouldn't tell that boyfriend of yours anything.

He's not the mole. You know full well I've been down that road and it's a dead-end.

It's just that—

And stop calling him my boyfriend, you prick.
You don't see it, Kate, but something doesn't add up with that guy and . . . .

The conversation ended and the crackling noise came back. Martindale rubbed his forehead with the fingers of both hands. The pounding in his head grew worse, making the room spin.

The crackling stopped, and then . . .

She drives a bright red Mini, registration YZZ 997, and she will be at Julio's Nightclub sometime after ten. Do you have the vial?

The voice was male and British.

Yes, ten grams of pure ethanol. Are you sure it will do the job?

A different voice. American?

The music resumed.

Ten minutes later, having stopped and started the tape several times, Martindale was sure there were no more hidden messages to find. He ejected the cassette, stood and tried to slide it into the front pocket of his jeans. But he couldn't. His right arm draped lifelessly by his side, refusing to comply with the simplest of commands. Eyes down, he witnessed the cassette slip through his fingers, hit the floor and bounce deep under the desk. He moved back a pace and right away, his right leg began its own protest. 'What the hell . . . .' He reached out for the arm of the chair to stop himself from falling, but grasped instead its ghostly double.

Part III

*T*wo days after Whitlam denounced the CIA for interfering in Australian internal affairs, President Gerald Ford fired CIA Director William Colby. It had been decided, principally by Dr Henry Kissinger, that Colby was telling Congress too much. Republican stalwart, George H.W. Bush, replaced him.

Kissinger's worries did not stop there. Two days later still the House Intelligence Committee subpoenaed him for details of American covert intelligence operations, including details of Soviet compliance with the nuclear arms agreement. Kissinger knew that Merino was vital to monitoring Soviet missile tests, and his fear that Whitlam might soon terminate Merino's lease grew daily.

No one at Langley was quite sure how much Whitlam knew. Colby, serving out his final days in office before the official handover of power, gambled that Whitlam's speech at Alice Springs was more bluster than anything else and issued a statement that Richard Stallings—Merino's first director—was not an agent of the CIA. But his gamble backfired. It was Friday 7th November, and by this time Whitlam had extracted the names of all CIA agents working in Australia from a reluctant Sir Arthur Tange, Head of the Australian Defence Department. Stallings' name was on the list.

The Deputy Director of the CIA's covert action division, Theodore G. Shackley, received several frantic cables from Canberra warning him that the determination of the Opposition to force a general election was weakening, while the public's support for Whitlam was growing.

Meanwhile, at an installation ten miles outside Melbourne, the intelligence unit of Australia's Defence Department played host to a visit by Governor-General Kerr. Kerr was briefed about the American base at Alice Springs and told of its vital role in the top-secret satellite spy operation, code-named Rhyolite. He was also told that if Whitlam remained Prime Minister, Australia risked being ejected from the 'Five Eyes' group for sharing signals intelligence. The 'Five Eyes' in question were Australia, Canada, New Zealand, the United Kingdom and the United States. After the briefing, Kerr flew back to Canberra for a pre-arranged meeting with Sir Garfield Barwick—Australia's Chief Justice—on the legality of dismissing Prime Minister Whitlam. Barwick did not hold back and told Kerr that, given the money supply crisis, it was his constitutional duty to dismiss Whitlam.

28. Muffins and madmen

Monday 10th November, Canberra

Confident that Whitlam's dismissal was a foregone conclusion, Walker prepared for his return to England and did so with glee. After almost two years in Australia, he longed for the comforts of his cosy stone cottage in the Cotswolds, for a pot of tea brewed with a fuss and served in fine china, for the occasional cold, grey day, and for a copy of *The Times* on the day it was printed.

There were bags to pack, receipts to organise and documents to shred, but all that could wait a little longer. Walker's most pressing task that Monday morning was to place on canvas the brilliant-blue November sky that hung over the city. He dispatched Jenny to *One-Stop Art Supplies* for a fresh tube of cerulean, and waited for her by the pool with muffins, coffee and suntan lotion for company.

'That was quick,' Walker called as Jenny appeared on the steps to the garden. He sat upright on a sun lounger, resting a mug of coffee between his legs.

Jenny walked down the steps and across the trimmed lawn to the pool's edge. 'I haven't gone yet,' she said at last. The morning sun was behind her.

'Why not?' Walker asked, shielding his eyes.

'Some bloke's parked right in front of the gate. He said he wanted to see you.'

'Does this *bloke* have a name?'

'He wouldn't tell me.'

'What does he look like?'

'Fat.'

'Fat, eh?' Walker replied with a controlled chuckle. 'Your candour, young lady, is a treasure I will miss.'

She fired a malignant smile at him.

'Is there anything else you can tell me about this portly gentleman?'

'He's American. And he's deaf.'

'Oh, Christ,' Walker said, his voice one key lower. 'Is anyone else with him?'

'No.'

Walker relaxed back into the sun lounger.

'I thought his head was going to explode when I told him to wait,' Jenny said. 'Should I bring him here?'

'Yes. But not through the house.'

When they emerged from around the side of the garage complex, Farnsworth was trailing Jenny by several feet. She stopped at the patio's edge, pointed towards the pool and then darted up the back stairs.

Without lifting his head from the lounger, Walker called after her. 'Cerulean, remember—a large tube, please.'

She acknowledged with a half-turn. Then she was gone.

Farnsworth stomped across the lawn and stood mute in front of Walker, out of breath and sweaty. Two empty chairs were close by but he remained standing.

Arms folded across his chest, Walker gazed at the sky. 'Did anyone see you arrive?'

'Good morning to you, too.'

'You've come a long way,' Walker said, still eyeing the sky. 'Why didn't you phone if you needed to speak with me? I thought the line was clean now.'

'Clean or not, I'm here. The least you could do is look at me.'

Walker did so, casually scanning Farnsworth's girth. 'Jenny was right,' he mumbled.

'What?'

'Nothing.' Walker planted a leg either side of the lounger and sat up. 'Have you found the recording?'

'We're still looking.'

'You do realise how damaging it could be?'

'I *said* we are still looking.'

'Then let us hope you find it soon.'

'We can handle it.'

'Like you handled Martindale?' Walker offered.

'No doubt MI6 would have done a better job,' Farnsworth replied.

'Yes, quite probably. But we don't do that sort of thing anymore.'

'Oh, yeah, I forgot. You guys get the French to do all your wet work these days.'

Walker tutted, his face sour with irritation. 'Was there any particular reason for this visit? I'm rather busy.'

'You look it.'

Walker groaned.

'I'm here to tell you,' Farnsworth said, 'that your time's up with this Governor-General crap.'

Walker's toes curled and his heart rate quickened. Leaning to one side, he swapped his coffee for a muffin, unwrapped its paper casing with pinched fingers and took a hefty bite.

'Did you hear what I said, Walker?'

An upturned mouth and short grunt were all that Walker offered. He gobbled down the mouthful.

'Look here, if you don't—'

'All right, keep your trousers on,' Walker interrupted. 'I take it *Operation Pineapples* is back on.'

'It was never off.'

Walker popped the rest of the muffin into his mouth and swallowed it whole. 'Why don't you sit down so that we can discuss this?'

Other than wiping the stagnant sweat from his brow, Farnsworth did not move. 'There's nothing to discuss,' he said. 'Just keep out of my way.'

'I fully intend to. Tell me . . . what are planning to do?'

'Whitlam has the deep-cover list of agents working here,' Farnsworth said, 'and we can't risk him identifying any more assets. He's already identified Stallings.'

'Actually,' Walker remarked, 'it was a reporter from the *Financial Times* that named Stallings, not the Prime Minister. And it was Doug Anthony himself who confirmed the story.'

'I don't give a rat's ass who confirmed it.'

'Sit down, Farnsworth, and let me explain what's going to happen?'

'I'm not staying.'

'Please sit down.' Walker offered a placating smile and a guiding hand.

After a second or two, Farnsworth let his weight fall into the nearest chair, cementing its legs deep in the soil. 'We have sound

Intel,' he said, 'that Whitlam intends to expose Merino in Parliament tomorrow afternoon.'

'I'm aware of that.'

'Are you? Well, while you've been sunning yourself by the pool, I've been busy doing something about it.'

Walker threw back a cold, unblinking stare. 'What have you done, exactly?'

'I cabled Ted Shackley to let him know—'

'*Jesus Christ.*' With a flush of energy, Walker swung his right leg over the sun lounger and stood, looking down on Farnsworth. 'You do realise, don't you, that Shackley is a veritable madman. That fellow is wound tighter than an idiot's watch, and there is no telling what he will do.'

Farnsworth stood also, his face a mirror of Walker's irritation. 'Shackley is the—'

'If Whitlam gets wind that the Governor-General's involved, everything I have worked for will be ruined.'

'Let Whitlam give his little speech in Parliament tomorrow,' Farnsworth snapped, 'and this whole damn mess will come crashing down on your head. Kissinger and Colby both denied Stallings was an agent. If Whitlam talks, he'll be calling them liars.'

With contempt dripping from every word, Walker said, 'Goodness, imagine the cheek of labelling those two as liars.'

'Think this is funny, eh? There is more at stake here than just Merino?'

'Indeed. Why do you think MI6 agreed to be involved in the first place? I can assure you it wasn't to save your precious little desert hideaway.'

'Then you understand why we can't let Whitlam talk,' Farnsworth said.

'And your considered proposal is to simply knock him off?'

'That's correct. And ASIO better get back on board if they know what's good for them.'

'I would tread carefully with Australian Security if I were you,' Walker said. 'It is probably the one Service on this planet where our agents are outstripped by the number of Russians.'

'With or without them, we're going ahead.'

'Has Langley approved the action, or is this just Shackley talking?' Walker asked.

'It's my call now,' Farnsworth replied. 'Everything's set for the morning.'

Walker's frown mutated to a teeth-baring artic scowl. 'Can you at least wait until the afternoon?'

Farnsworth's chest heaved. 'No.'

'Just hear me out . . . *please.*' Walker took a steadying breath. 'Whitlam is not going to get the opportunity to reveal anything tomorrow. Kerr will dismiss him and he will do it *before* the House opens. It is the only solution guarantying cover for all of us.'

Farnsworth's face puckered. 'You're on another planet if you believe that will happen.'

'What I believe, Farnsworth, is that my plan is infinitely neater than blowing Whitlam's brains out.'

'That's not how we're going to do it.'

'Oh, exploding cigars, is it?'

'Look here, you smug son-of-a-bitch. For your information, we have a cast-iron method that won't leave any trail back to us.'

'All I'm asking for is a few hours,' Walker pressed.

'What's your problem?' Farnsworth said. 'You were quite happy for that Hamilton girl to be knocked off.'

'She was a two-bit reporter, not a Head of State. *Operation Pineapples* is insane. And if you go through with it, you'll be doing so on your own. MI6 won't support you and neither will Langley.'

'The operation was—'

'If you think approval from Shackley is enough, I can only assume you are as mad as he is. Shackley is operating outside the system and has been for some time. The new regime at Langley will not sanction an assassination, and you bloody well know it.'

The vein in Farnsworth's right temple was standing proud and pulsed like a hungry worm.

'*Well*?' Walker said.

Stiffly, Farnsworth stepped back a pace. After some heavy breathing and an erratic face twitch, he snapped his chin up and declared, 'You have until one o'clock—not a minute longer.'

'That will do nicely.' Walker's smile seemed almost genuine. 'Thank you.'

Farnsworth left without hesitation and was nearing the side exit when Walker called after him, 'Be a good chap and close the gate on your way out.'

29. The dismissal

Theodore G. Shackley's *raison d'être* was ensuring that the leaders of "friendly" governments stayed in power while those of "unfriendly" governments were deposed. Shackley made his name in black operations, first as head of CIA's terror programme against Fidel Castro, then as the Station Chief in Saigon directing the agency's secret war in Vietnam. His handiwork was also evident in Iran, Afghanistan and Angola.

The Australian Labor Government had been part of Shackley's portfolio for some time, but it was not until the second weekend of November 1975 that "the Whitlam problem" reached the top of his agenda. The tipping point was a string of cables from Farnsworth, the last and most alarming of which read, 'WHITLAM SET TO EXPOSE MERINO IN PARLIAMENT ON 11/11'. Shackley scratched out a reply and ordered the Australian intelligence representative in Washington to send it on a strict service-to-service link to the Director-General of the Australian Security Intelligence Organisation (ASIO) in Canberra.

Unlike his predecessor, newly appointed Director-General Frank J. Mahoney was not of the opinion that ASIO should be beholden to the CIA ahead of the Australian Prime Minister. Mahoney received Shackley's cable on the morning of Monday 10

November and handed it to Whitlam at Tullamarine Airport that very afternoon. It read:

ON 2 NOVEMBER THE PM OF AUSTRALIA MADE A STATEMENT AT ALICE SPRINGS TO THE EFFECT THAT THE CIA HAD BEEN FUNDING DOUG ANTHONY'S NATIONAL COUNTRY PARTY IN AUSTRALIA.

ON 4 NOVEMBER THE U.S. EMBASSY IN AUSTRALIA CATEGORICALLY DENIED THAT CIA HAD GIVEN MONEY TO THE NATIONAL COUNTRY PARTY OR ITS LEADER.

AT THIS STAGE CIA WAS DEALING ONLY WITH THE STALLINGS INCIDENT AND WAS ADOPTING A NO COMMENT ATTITUDE IN THE HOPE THAT THE MATTER WOULD BE GIVEN LITTLE OR NO PUBLICITY. STALLINGS IS A RETIRED CIA EMPLOYEE.

ON 6 NOVEMBER THE PRIME MINISTER PUBLICALLY REPEATED THE ALLEGATION THAT HE KNEW OF TWO INSTANCES IN WHICH CIA MONEY HAD BEEN USED TO INFLUENCE DOMESTIC AUSTRALIAN POLITICS. PRESS COVERAGE WAS SUCH THAT A NUMBER OF CIA MEMBERS SERVING IN AUSTRALIA HAVE BEEN IDENTIFIED. IT IS NOT POSSIBLE NOW FOR CIA TO CONTINUE TO DEAL WITH THE MATTER ON A NO COMMENT BASIS.

ON 7 NOVEMBER, FIFTEEN NEWSPAPER OR WIRE SERVICE REPS CALLED THE PENTAGON SEEKING INFORMATION ON THE ALLEGATIONS MADE IN AUSTRALIA.

CIA CANNOT SEE HOW THIS DIALOGUE WITH CONTINUED REFERENCE TO CIA CAN DO OTHER THAN

BLOW THE LID OFF THOSE INSTALLATIONS WHERE THE PERSONS CONCERNED HAVE BEEN WORKING, PARTICULARLY THE INSTALLATION AT ALICE SPRINGS.

ON 7 NOVEMBER AT A PRESS CONFERENCE, COLBY WAS ASKED WHETHER THE ALLEGATIONS MADE IN AUSTRALIA WERE TRUE. HE CATEGORICALLY DENIED THEM.

THIS MESSAGE SHOULD BE REGARDED AS AN OFFICIAL DÉMARCHE ON A SERVICE-TO-SERVICE LINK. CIA FEELS THAT IF THIS PROBLEM CANNOT BE SOLVED THEY DO NOT SEE HOW OUR MUTUALLY BENEFICIAL RELATIONSHIPS ARE GOING TO CONTINUE.

THE CIA FEELS GRAVE CONCERN AS TO WHERE THIS TYPE OF PUBLIC DISCUSSION MAY LEAD. THE DIRECTOR-GENERAL SHOULD BE ASSURED THAT CIA DOES NOT LIGHTLY ADOPT THIS ATTITUDE.

Whitlam read the whole cable in silence, and then re-read one sentence aloud. 'This message should be regarded as an official démarche on a service-to-service link.'

'You weren't meant to see it, Gough,' said Mahoney.

'Clearly not.' Whitlam held the cable close, his face a mix of bewilderment and alarm. 'I wonder what George would make of it.'

'Doug Anthony's spitting bullets that his name is being dragged through the mud,' Mahoney said. 'He's expecting a statement from you in the House to clear his name.'

'Does he, indeed?' Whitlam waved the cable. 'I'll give him a statement to chew on.'

*

Prime Minister Edward Gough Whitlam never delivered his statement. An hour before the House sat the following day, Tuesday 11 November 1975, Governor-General Sir John Kerr dismissed Whitlam. The exchange of words between the two men was brief, as was Kerr's letter of dismissal. It read:

Government House, Canberra, 2600.
11 November 1975

Dear Mr Whitlam,
In accordance with section 64 of the Constitution, I hereby determine your appointment as my Chief Adviser and Head of the Government. It follows that I also hereby determine the appointments of all of the Ministers in your government.

You have previously told me that you would never resign or advise an election of the House of Representatives or a double dissolution and that the only way in which such an election could be obtained would be by my dismissal of you and your ministerial colleagues. As it appeared likely that you would today persist in this attitude I decided that, if you did, I would determine your commission and state my reasons for doing so. You have persisted in your attitude and I have accordingly acted as indicated. I attach a statement of my reasons, which I intend to publish immediately.

It is with a great deal of regret that I have taken this step both in respect of yourself and your colleagues.

I propose to send for the Leader of the Opposition and to commission him to form a new caretaker government until an election can be held.

Yours sincerely,
John R. Kerr

The Leader of the Opposition, Malcolm Fraser, did not have far to come. He was waiting in the room next door.

Stephen J Anderson

30. Lizard Island

Lizard Island, Great Barrier Reef

Martindale's only regular companion during his stay on Lizard Island was a lizard. Each morning, soon after sunrise, the same tail-wagging, tongue-probing, yellow-spotted creature appeared on the front porch of his seaside bungalow. At least, Martindale assumed it was the same creature and not a succession of lookalike cousins.

The young woman in Reception did little to hide her amusement at Martindale's fear of the lizard. 'This *is* Lizard Island,' she giggled down the phone, adding, 'It must be a juvenile if it's only two feet long.' This particular news did little to allay his concern and he asked her what he should do. 'Give 'em eggs,' came the sassy instruction.

And so each morning for two weeks, Sam—as he or she came to be known—was given a hearty breakfast of eggs. And toast. And mushrooms. Convinced that Sam would also enjoy munching on a finger or two, Martindale served each course from behind a barrier of oversized clay pots.

Aside from lizards, the tiny Coral Sea island enjoyed the company of pythons, tree snakes, green turtles and the odd flying fox. Its human inhabitants consisted almost entirely of young couples and newlyweds. Children were rare. Single males were rarer still.

Martindale was alone on the island, and happily so. The brochure's promise of "a land secluded from the rest of the world" was just what he needed. His routine was set from day two: Rise at daybreak. Feed Sam. A brisk walk along the beach. Coffee at Pebbles Bar. Snorkeling over the reef. Back to Pebbles for a "triple-decker" sandwich and light beer. Late afternoon sail. Evening swim in the hotel pool. And dinner, alone, in his bungalow.

Before arriving on the island, Martindale thought he might never sail again— nightmares centred on the murky waters of Lake Burley Griffin were the problem. But the speed and grace of a Hobie 14 Catamaran on the open water lit a fire in his belly. Each afternoon's sailing brought back treasured memories, including the first on-the-water lesson from his father.

On his last full day, he dispensed with lunch—except for the beer—to enjoy more quality daylight on the water. He headed east, further out to sea than on any previous day, further than the rental company allowed, further than his nautical skills permitted. Behind, only the mountainous tip of Lizard Island was visible. Ahead, the sea grew vast and uneven. He clocked the height of the sun and carried on. Soon, Lizard was gone and so too were the breaking waters over the reef and the playful company of a lone osprey. The wind now punched the sail with anger; salt spray dug into his eyes. Finally, when his feelings of fear and liberty were about equal, he turned the boat about.

Wednesday 12 November

One final breakfast with Sam and it was time to join the world again.

Duffle bag in hand, Martindale strolled along the beach to Reception for the orange minibus to the island's airstrip. The flight to Cairns left in thirty minutes. A connecting flight to Canberra would see him home by six.

The flight attendant on board Hinterland's single-engine Cessna greeted Martindale with a toothy smile and that day's copy of *The Sydney Morning Herald*. Having avoided newspapers and television during his retreat, he was unaware of events back home. All events except one, that is—no one on the island escaped the news of Whitlam's dismissal.

Buckled up for take-off, he kicked off his shoes and began reading. The first few pages were devoted almost exclusively to candid photographs of Whitlam, Kerr and Fraser. Whitlam's chest was puffed out as usual, but his eyes were unfocused and lost. Fraser had his chin aloft with a born-to-rule smile on his face. Kerr had the look of a rabbit trapped in the headlights of a road-train. Martindale skimmed the articles with moderate interest. Buffoons, all of them, he thought.

He turned another page expecting more tedious arguments on the future of the land down under. But what he got was an article that cut right through his chest, leaving him struggling to breathe. It began "*The Special Adviser to the Prime Minister, Professor George Martindale, remains in a critical condition in the Royal*

Canberra Hospital, having collapsed in his office at Parliament House from a suspected stroke ten days ago."

Martindale wiped away a tear. On the journey across to the mainland, he only uttered one word: Dad.

31. The hum of spying

That same morning

Palmer was woken at seven fifteen with a bowl of buckwheat porridge, cottage cheese pancakes, black tea and a pretty smile. An hour later that same pretty smile escorted him to the secure communications room, deep in the building's basement. One guard was outside the room and another was inside, standing against the piles of electronic gadgetry that lined its walls.

With the artful stare of a teenager viewing top-shelf magazines, Palmer looked around the room at the multitude of dials, wires and miniature light bulbs, all testimony to the hum of spying that filled his ears. A ceiling-mounted extractor fan competed well with the persistent hum, but did little to quell the room's unique aroma of heated conduit and freshly redistributed dust.

The young woman pointed to a lone chair at one end of a wooden table, upon which sat more gadgetry, that morning's *Sydney Morning Herald* and a foolscap-sized envelope with Palmer's name emblazoned across it in capital letters.

Palmer blinked hard at his name.

'Comrade Dobrogorskiy will be with you soon,' she said. 'You must sit now.'

He obliged, stretching his legs under the table.

The young woman paid him a demure bow and left.

Palmer watched the door close and then leaned forward and took hold of the envelope.

'*Nyet!*' the guard said with a lively shake of his head.

'It has my name on it.' Palmer's tone implied custody was rightly his.

'*Nyet.*'

Keeping his eyes on the guard, Palmer gently bounced the envelope up and down in mid-air for a few thorny seconds, then let it go. 'What about the paper? May I read the paper?'

Before the guard could answer, the door opened and Dobrogorskiy walked in.

The guard cracked to attention, bringing his right hand, palm down, to his right temple. '*Ser.*'

Palmer sat up and drew his feet under the chair. His eyes locked on the old man's wooden cane. Was he using a walking stick in the children's park?

With the smallest flick of his head, Dobrogorskiy dismissed the guard, who returned another salute and left.

The old man moved forward, rested a hand on Palmer's upper back and said, with a paternal smile, 'Did you sleep well?'

'Thank you, yes.' Palmer voice was thin and a little shaky.

'And how was your Russian breakfast?'

'It was very nice,' Palmer answered, aware of letting his body unwind.

'Excellent.' Dobrogorskiy withdrew his hand from Palmer's back. 'Then we can begin.' He lifted his cane and planted its tip on the envelope. 'Have you read this?'

'No.'

He slid the cane across to the newspaper and tapped it once. 'This?'

'Only the headline.'

Dobrogorskiy voiced the spirited caption. 'Bulldog becomes the underdog.' After a short pause, he gave a belly-driven laugh. 'Tell me,' he said, tapping the paper twice more, 'what do you think your comrades at the CIA will make of this?'

Palmer shrugged. 'They'll be happy Whitlam's gone.'

'No, Mister Palmer, they will not be happy. Mister Whitlam has a great deal of sympathy now, and the good people of this land are angry—angry enough, I believe, to vote him back into office. That is what your comrades will determine, do you not think?'

Palmer looked again at the newspaper headline.

'Mister Palmer?'

Palmer cupped his jaw, pulling it down slightly as if his mouth needed to be pried open to speak. 'Maybe,' he said quietly.

With a nod to the envelope, Dobrogorskiy said, 'Please open it.'

Palmer did so, upending the contents into his hand—a few sheets of handwritten notes, hole-punched and tied together with a bow of blue ribbon.

'That is what we have on *Operation Pineapples*,' Dobrogorskiy explained. 'We need you to help us fill in some details.'

There was no response.

'You have heard of the plan, yes?'

'Yeah,' came Palmer's breathy acknowledgement, as though he was partly to blame for the plans very existence. 'After we spoke in the park I did some digging on my own. It's true that *Pineapples* was a plan to assassinate Whitlam. But it didn't mean anything. It was just some free-thinking by a few crazy technicians at Langley. The plan wasn't approved by the Director and ended up in the trashcan like most of their ideas. In any event,' he added, 'there has been a total regime change at CIA Headquarters.'

'We understand what is happening at Langley,' Dobrogorskiy said. 'Regrettably, Langley does not understand what is happening down here. *Operation Pineapples* is not in the trashcan, as you say. Please read the notes and you will see.'

Palmer flipped through the sheets of paper, scarcely focusing on a single word, and then set them down. 'Tell me about George Martindale.'

Dobrogorskiy twisted his head to one side and gently rubbed the back of his neck. He said nothing.

'If you want me to help you, Mister Dobrogorskiy, I need to know what *you* know. I'm not playing games here.'

'Nor are we, Mister Palmer.'

'Well, then?'

Dobrogorskiy gave a weak smile of assent and said, 'There is at least one other agent positioned within the government, and Professor Martindale is our chief suspect. To begin with, his background is very questionable: unremarkable childhood, a model student and celebrated academic, with no money problems and no trouble with the law.'

'That hardly qualifies him to be a spy,' Palmer quipped.

Dobrogorskiy had the bearing of a teacher who had just caught his star pupil making a silly remark. 'Young man, Professor Martindale's past is much too clean to be true.'

'Did he have anything to do with the death of his wife?' Palmer asked.

'Possibly.'

Palmer could feel the blood rise in his neck. 'Did he or didn't he?'

'We are not entirely sure what the professor is up to. Certainly, there is no question the premature death of his lovers is irregular—he is either very unlucky or he is somehow involved in this whole affair.'

'I saw how upset he was when Kate Hamilton died,' Palmer said. 'He *couldn't* have had anything to do with her accident.'

'Even so, I think it is best we keep a watchful eye on Professor Martindale, assuming he ever leaves the hospital. For the moment, our most important task is to keep Mister Whitlam out of danger. Then, if the Gods are smiling, he may soon be re-elected as Prime Minister.'

'What is it that you want me to do?'

'We believe the Governor-General's actions were driven by the American and British intelligence services. If we can secure strong evidence for this, we could use it to our advantage. Please see the notes. We have some audio recordings for you as well. Someone will be along in a short while to arrange everything for you.' Dobrogorskiy reached out and tapped Palmer's shoulder twice in quick succession. 'We will talk again in one hour.'

For a few minutes, Palmer was alone in the bowels of the Soviet Embassy with nothing to do other than wrestle with his thoughts. Was he a guest or a prisoner, a hero or a traitor, brave or stupid? The answers changed from one moment to the next with the frequency of a bee's wings.

32. Father and son

Early evening, that same day

The Department of Critical Care was as dire as its name suggested. No one spoke. No one smiled. All doors were closed. All curtains were drawn. The lights were blinding. The décor was dull. The only sounds were crying and the wheeze of an unseen mechanical pump. The only smells were disinfectant and death.

As Tim Martindale approached the receptionist, she disappeared behind a row of filing cabinets. He was constrained to watch the misery on display in the waiting area nearby. In the far corner, an elderly couple sat hand in hand. Both were weeping. Two seats along, a young man in stained overalls was doubled over with his head buried in his hands. A police officer was sitting next to him; an empty baby's car seat was on the floor by their feet. A young couple stood nearby—she with a brave face, he struggling to stay upright.

The receptionist reappeared with a handful of patient folders and deposited them in a cart by the desk. 'May I help you?' she asked.

'I've come to see my father, George Martindale. I telephoned earlier.'

She ran her finger down a page of names on the desk, quickly checked a wall clock and said, 'If you would like to take a seat, Doctor Cummings will be with you soon.'

*

A fifty-plus, grey-haired man introduced himself to Tim and then promptly led him to a small lounge area kitted out with shabby armchairs, a coffee table and a thin rack of medical journals—the *Annals of Critical Care* figured prominently. Stale tobacco smoke and lavender air freshener cushioned the tang of bleach within the room.

'Please take a seat, Mister Martindale.'

Tim remained standing. 'I would have come sooner but I've been away and—'

'Your timing's perfect—your father was in a coma until last night.'

'*Coma?*'

'A drug-induced coma. That's quite different from—'

'I thought he had a stroke.'

'We did consider that.'

Tim screwed up his face. 'Did he have a stroke or not?'

'He didn't.'

'So . . . he's all right?'

'Yes, your father's doing well now.'

'Can I see him?'

'Of course, but I need to explain a couple of things first.' The doctor tapped the backrest of a nearby armchair. 'Please take a seat.'

They both sat.

'This was kept out of the newspapers,' the doctor said, 'and I don't want to alarm you, but . . . someone attacked your father.'

'Attacked?' Tim repeated slowly, as though trying to make sense of the word. 'In Parliament House?'

'No, he drove there after the attack. Though quite how he managed to do that given his condition is anyone's guess.'

'What happened?' Tim asked.

'He was hit hard several times on the back of the head. To be honest, it's a miracle his skull wasn't fractured.' With a grin, the doctor added, 'I didn't think professors could have such thick heads.'

Tim roused a bleak smile. 'Who did it?'

'No one knows. Your father doesn't remember much and the police don't have anything to go on. They're working on the assumption it was a simple robbery, but that's not what it looks like to me. For starters, your father still had his wallet on him when he arrived here, with plenty of cash in it.'

'I don't understand.'

'Join the club. All I can tell you is that whoever hit your father wasn't just trying to knock him out—one of the blows was extremely heavy. Personally, I think someone was trying to kill him . . . or at least cause him significant harm.'

Tim's eyes widened. 'Did you say that to the police?'

'Yes. I also told the Secret Service, but no one seemed particularly interested. It was quite odd.'

Tim shook his head.

'In any case the heavy blow caused your father's brain to swell, and we induced a coma to allow time for everything to settle down. I'm happy to say it all worked fine and your father came out of it without any complications. He still has a drip in for nutrients. Other than that, all he needs is bed rest and aspirin.'

'No brain damage?' Tim said.

'We need to keep him under observation for a while, but we're not expecting any permanent effects. All being well, your father should be on his feet in a day or two. His legs might be a bit wobbly, but he'll be all right.'

'Does he know what happened yesterday?' Tim asked.

'Sorry?'

'About Mister Whitlam.'

'Oh . . . I don't know.'

'Should I tell him?'

'Yes, if you want. He needs to know sometime.'

*

The private room at the far end of the department had all the appeal of an inner city bus station in winter. Martindale was half-sitting, half-lying in the narrow bed, anchored to it by an intravenous drip and the burden of a weeklong coma. His unshaven face and bruised cheek gave him an appearance of somewhere between rugged explorer and degenerate tramp.

Tim viewed the spectacle from just inside the room. In place of a voiced greeting, he raised his chin and furnished a straight-lipped smile.

Martindale responded to the offering, such as it was, with a beaming smile and a warm hello. He extended his arm towards a chair by the bed.

Tim lumbered forward, pulled the chair a little farther away from the bed and sat down.

'You look well,' Martindale said, his voice weak and raspy.

'You don't.'

'No, I guess not.'

'So what happened?' Tim asked.

'I got mugged.'

'Really? Doctor Cummings thought someone was trying to knock you off.'

'Yeah, well, Doctor Cummings has an active imagination.'

'Did you—'

'You've got a good tan,' Martindale interrupted. 'Where have you been?'

'Lizard Island.'

'With Julie?'

'No. We broke up a month ago.'

'I'm sorry to hear that. She was a lovely girl from what I saw.'

'I'm over it,' Tim said with a healthy dollop of irritation. He dropped his eyes to the marbled floor.

To cover the awkward silence, Martindale took a sip of water from the bedside stand and joked, 'I don't think I've ever drunk so much water.'

Tim's gaze did not leave the floor.

The stillness between them was all-consuming until, finally, Martindale said, 'I miss her too.'

When he looked up, Tim's face had gone from indifferent to shattered; his eyes glistened with mounting fluid.

'I'm sorry, Tim, believe me. But please . . . I don't want to lose you as well.'

Tim stood abruptly, driving the chair back with his legs. 'Why did she have to die?'

'If I could turn back the clock—'

'You never cared about mum.' Tim's voice cracked with anger. 'I knew you wanted a divorce.'

'You're wrong, Tim, it wasn't like that. We had our ups and downs but—'

'Did you want her dead as well?'

'*Tim!* That's a ridiculous thing to say. You don't know what you're talking about.'

'I know there was nothing wrong with that fucking boat.'

'Sit down, will you?'

'I don't give a shit what you've told anyone else, but the least you could do is tell me the truth. I could smell the mint on your breath that night. Did you think I didn't know what it meant? I knew just as well as mum did.'

'All right, that's enough.'

'It was your fault and I want to hear you say it.'

'Yes, it was my fault,' Martindale said, spitting the words out as a final apology. 'Now sit down and we can talk.'

Tim continued to stand. 'How'd you get away with it?'

'It's complicated. You'll have to trust me on that.'

'*Trust you?*' Tim spewed with the temper of a trapped dog. 'How can I trust you? It's taken you all this time to admit you were drunk, and even then you only said it because you're dying here in this godforsaken place.'

'Am I dying?' came the deadpan retort. Martindale's head sank deeper into the pillow.

Tim looked on for a long moment. Then, with an energetic tug, he pulled the chair back close to the bed. He flopped into it and wiped his cheek with a sweep of his fingers.

'Thank you,' Martindale mouthed. 'As soon I can, Tim, I'm going to resign as Adviser and go back to teaching. With a bit of luck, my life might resemble something approaching normal again.'

'Do you even have a job in politics anymore?'

'Why do you say that?'

'Whitlam got the sack yesterday.'

Martindale lifted his head a little. 'No one can sack the Prime Minister.'

'You might try telling that to the Governor-General.'

Martindale flinched, catching the intravenous drip on the bedclothes. Pain flew up his arm and exploded across his face.

'Ouch,' Tim said.

Martindale nudged the blanket away from the needle. 'So the bastards actually did it,' he said with a voice hovering between guilt and defeat.

'Did what?'

'Never mind. What excuse did Kerr give?'

'Whitlam's failure to secure supply. Fraser's been appointed caretaker PM until the election.'

'When?'

'December thirteenth.'

Staring at the bare wall opposite, Martindale gave no indication he heard the reply.

Tim glanced at the same wall, shrugged, and said, 'Anyway, I have to go.' He stood. 'Maybe I'll come back in a day or two.'

Martindale sat up. 'I need you to do something for me.'

'Like what?'

'Disappear for a week or two.'

Tim's head jerked backwards.

'I can't explain why,' Martindale said, 'but—'

'What are you talking about? I'm not going to—'

'There's something I need to do, and I don't want you to get hurt as a result.'

'It wasn't a mugging, was it?'

'No, it wasn't.'

Tim's face was taut; his eyes unblinking. 'You mean someone was really trying to kill you?'

Martindale reached across to the bedside cabinet and took out his wallet. 'I can't tell you anything at the moment because there are important security issues. I'm sorry, but that's the way it is.'

'What are you,' Tim said with a stifled laugh, 'some kind of spy?'

Martindale opened the wallet and extracted all the cash. 'Take this.' He held out his hand. 'There's almost two hundred dollars there.'

Tim stared at the money for a second or two, and then stuffed it into the front of his jeans. 'What am I supposed to do with it?'

'Do you remember that rundown camping place we stayed at a couple of years ago, the one near Mudgee?'

'How could I forget it?'

'You need to get yourself there without anyone knowing, and stay there until I contact you. Leave your car at home and go by coach.'

'Jesus, you're serious.'

'Don't register in your own name and don't write any cheques. Two hundred dollars should go a long way in that place.'

'Who's going to hurt me?'

'No one, I hope, but I don't want to take any chances.'

'So who are you spying for?'

'Please, Tim . . . .'

'Someone tried to kill you, and now you expect me to go into hiding with no questions asked. Are you crazy?'

'Certifiable, I should think.'

'If you want me to—'

'I won't ask any more of you, Tim, I promise. But this one time, I need you to do as I say.'

Tim paused before asking, 'Will you ever tell me the truth?'

Martindale's face gave nothing away. 'I'll be with you soon as I can.'

With his son gone, Martindale looked around the room and the few things in it. There were probably more depressing places to be, but he couldn't think of any. He settled back and stared at the ceiling. With cold, dead eyes, he said, 'Now it's my turn.'

33. Chasing taillights

The following day, Thursday 13 November

Ten days of drug-fuelled oblivion had turned Martindale's legs into malevolent strangers. His first attempt at walking ended with a loud obscenity and the clash of metal on marble. The nurse found him spread-eagled on the floor, the intravenous drip lying beside him. She withdrew the needle from the back of his hand, checked that nothing was broken and settled him back into bed. After a pithy reprimand, which he accepted freely, she dispensed more aspirin and an efficient—though agreeable—massage. He promised to stay in bed. She promised a breakfast of toast, tea and fruit.

She kept her word.

He did not.

Clutching the few straws of health on offer—no bleeding, no ringing in the ears, no dizziness—Martindale worked his pig-headed legs with short trips around the bedroom. An awkward shuffle soon progressed to a confident stagger. By two in the afternoon, the stagger was a stiff, flat-footed walk. Was it enough to get out of that wretched place? He hunched his shoulders. It would have to do. He eliminated the discreet view of his backside with a snug knot in the hospital gown, made his way to the Duty Sister and stated his intention to leave.

With matchless confidence, the Sister warned of the dangers posed by leaving the hospital too soon. Martindale signed the "discharged against medical advice" form soon after.

*

On entering the drab silence of his apartment, Martindale surveyed each room for signs of his recent uninvited visitor. Nothing seemed disturbed or out of place.

Showered and shaved, he lent across the sink to bring his face into sharp focus in the bathroom mirror. 'Shit,' he said as a summary to both his looks and his life. He subdued the yellow-edged bruises on his cheek with a few dabs of talcum powder, gave his contacts a much needed clean, and walked through to the bedroom to complete his magic act with a white shirt, dark blue suit and sombre tie. He then dialled for a taxi to Parliament House and left to wait downstairs. It was seven o'clock.

*

Martindale spotted his Toyota Corolla still parked in its designated space. The spaces for Whitlam, Fraser and Anthony's cars were empty, but otherwise the car park was full.

To avoid Kings Hall and its associated hangers-on, he entered the House via the Cabinet Room's courtyard. From there he passed through to the Prime Minister's lobby.

Fingers of neon light poked out from beneath Mrs Henderson's closed door. As she rarely left before ten, Martindale was not surprised to see her lights on. But he was surprised to see her door

179

shut and accepted his good fortune with a fly-by through the lobby, nonstop to his office.

A musty odour and a few furtive glances around the room lifted his hopes that nothing had been disturbed. He walked behind his desk and, using the chair for support, went down on his knees. He scowled as a nagging ache spread through his legs, flooding his lower back with pins and needles. Maybe he should have heeded the Sister's advice.

With one last push, he bent down with his head near the floor and focussed deep under the desk. The moment his eyes adjusted to the shadows, his cheek brushed the carpet with a broad smile.

*

Martindale turned the key and gave quiet encouragement to his Corolla as it laboured free from a two-week slumber. The dashboard clock read seven fifty. He drove out of the car park and headed west for the suburb of Yarralumla.

Turning right off the highway, he went a thousand yards down a narrow tree-lined road, slowing to a crawl before a bend to the left. A flag of royal blue and gold flying at full mast was visible above the treetops. Now what does he do? His nerves fluttering like a wind-blown leaf, he pulled onto the gravel by the side of the road and switched off the engine.

Martindale had visited Governor-General Sir John Kerr at Government House on at least a dozen occasions, but only by invitation and usually as an adjunct to Prime Minister Whitlam. Would an unannounced visit be welcome? He put his chances at fifty-fifty.

And if he was admitted, how should he begin: Challenging— *why did you dismiss the Prime Minister?* Conciliatory—*I think you made the right decision, Sir John.* Or curious—*have you been in contact with the Palace?*

Staring into the growing blackness of the night, his thoughts ran free: *Hey, Johnny. I was wondering, you're not by chance in cahoots with MI6 or the CIA, are you? It's just that I'm trying to locate an associate of mine, and a little bird tells me you might know where he lives. I'm fairly certain he works for MI6. He's definitely English—sixty-something, slim with white hair. Sound familiar? You see, Johnny, I think he organised the murder of my girlfriend, Kate. She was a reporter for Nine News. Smart as a whip. Cute as a button. But it seems she knew too much. You know how it goes. Anyway, Johnny, do you know him? Do you know where I could find that slimy English cunt?*

A beam of light speared the gum trees to his right, breaking his reverie. A moment later, a Jaguar swung past and accelerated up the road. The driver's head of white hair was easy enough to see, but it was too dark for Martindale to make out if anyone else was in the car.

In the time it took to snatch a breath of air, Martindale made the decision to follow the red taillights. His heart pounding like a blacksmith's hammer, he started the car, turned the wheel full lock and hurtled out of the gravel, sending a shower of stones in all directions.

Down a leafy lane in a plush part of Canberra, less than four miles from Government House, the Jaguar disappeared behind heavy iron gates and a high brick wall.

Martindale parked on the verge a little way down the lane, and gave the driver ten minutes to enter the property and settle in. Taking the pistol from the boot, he walked back to the gates and pried through the narrow vertical gap between them. The tarmac drive turned after a few yards, and whatever lay beyond was hidden behind trees and hedging. Looking up, his eyes met the steady gaze of a camera perched on a metal brace to the right of the gates. Teeth clenched, he grunted at the camera and walked on.

Further up the lane, he came to a willow tree growing close to the brick wall. Despite his gammy legs, he managed to scale the low branches and climb the wall with ease. But he landed with a thud, his ankle twisting sharply on a rock and his knees finding a sizeable patch of wet mushrooms. He clutched his ankle and made a cursory assessment of the damage. Bruised but not broken? He stood gingerly and brushed his hands. Looking down, he sneered at a clump of squashed mushroom stalks as it peeled away from his trousers.

Stepping out of the foliage, a white-painted, two-storey house appeared through the trees like a pop-up in a book. With a smile of undiluted malice, Martindale said, 'Showtime, Mister Walker.'

34. Dead weight

After gawking at the surveillance camera by the front gates, Martindale assumed his chance of achieving a surprise visit was already lost. In any event, given his general state of disrepair, he didn't fancy a concealed slog through rose beds, box hedging and a small coniferous forest. With a prayer that no guard dogs would be in pursuit, he resigned himself to a measured limp up the central path to the house.

He was thirty feet from the house when a mass of lights laid bare the path, himself and the surrounding lawn. He limped faster.

Upstairs was in darkness. Downstairs, the sash windows were lit and partially open—a stray thought of sneaking in through one of them was blinked away and he walked directly to the front door. He knocked twice, then pressed the buzzer for a length of time that was certain to be irritating. In the seconds that followed, he tested how easy it would be to reach for the pistol tucked into his trouser belt at the small of his back. Was the safety catch on? 'Don't blow your arse off, George,' he said quietly.

The door opened and the Englishman stood before him. After a stage of mute posturing by both men, Martindale said, 'For some reason, I never expected you to be the one answering the door.'

Walker stayed silent and made no gesture of any kind, other than to peer left and right past Martindale to the garden beyond.

'You don't seem pleased to see me,' Martindale said. 'I'm disappointed.'

'To be perfectly honest,' Walker replied, 'I was rather hoping you were dead.'

'Yes, I'm sure you were.'

Walker scanned Martindale from head to toe. 'What happened to your knees?' he asked.

'Mushrooms,' explained Martindale.

'Hmm . . . I suppose you had better come in,' Walker said, moving to one side. Before closing the door, he looked again at the lawn and bordering shrubbery.

Martindale scoured the scene before him: a grand entrance hall with a staircase ascending into the dark, its bottom step adorned with a neat stack of paperback books and a pair of brown corduroy slippers. Three large suitcases and a mid-sized duffel bag were bunched together on a central strip of red carpet. The door to the left was ajar. The door to the right was fully open—Mahler's Symphony number two coasted through. Both rooms were brightly illuminated.

'I assume that was you parked outside Government House,' Walker said.

'Correct. Visiting a friend, were you?'

'Where's your car?'

'Not far.'

'Were you tailed?'

Martindale shrugged. 'How would I know?'

'What do you want?' Walker asked.

'The truth would be nice.'

'You know the truth.'

With a glance to the luggage by the stairs, Martindale said, 'Going somewhere?'

'I'll ask again, shall I? What do you want?'

'Who else is in the house?'

'No one.'

'No one?' Martindale said with his eyebrows pinched. 'A big house like this and you expect me to believe no one else is here? No butler? No maid?'

'Believe what you want.'

'A little wife lurking in the background, perhaps?'

'*No*,' came Walker's reply with a snarl revealing the full measure of his irritation.

'What's the matter? You don't like women?'

Walker's sugar-sweet smile did little to mask the frown beneath. 'I am a patient man, Martindale, but it has been a tiresome day.'

'So I gathered.'

'Then please, if you wouldn't mind, tell me why you are here.'

'Very well.' Martindale reached inside his jacket.

Walker's back straightened.

'Relax,' Martindale said as he pulled the cassette free. 'This is a little present for you.' He held the cassette at eye level, gave it a spirited shake and said, 'Know what it is?'

'Should I?'

'It's my get out of jail card.'

'What?'

'Pass go, collect two hundred bucks and proceed direct to Marylebone Station.'

'You like to play games, do you, Professor?'

'Not as much as you do, I expect.'

Another shoddy smile from Walker, this time laced with a touch of the arctic cold. 'We had better go through to my study.'

'Sure . . . after you.'

Walker strode past Martindale and into the room where Mahler was playing.

Martindale followed, his eyes lingering on the darkness at the top of the stairs. He passed into the study still limping like a stray dog, and surveyed it with the unease of a thieving teenager.

Walker turned the music off and stood in front of his desk, facing Martindale. 'Sore leg, have we?'

'My leg's just fine.'

'Clearly.' Walker extended his right arm, palm up. 'May I listen to the tape?'

'Sure, catch,' Martindale replied, lobbing it at Walker.

Walker's head flung back while his hands jerked forward, fingers spread to net the cassette. He missed. The cassette clipped his chest and fell to the floor. Bending for it, he took a sharp intake of breath as his eyes touched on the back of a small picture frame on the desk. He picked up the cassette and stood. 'That was most kind of you.'

'Don't mention it.'

Walker went behind his desk and retrieved a chunky cassette player from the bottom drawer. He positioned the player in front of the picture frame, obscuring the photograph within it, and inserted the tape.

'Fast-forward twenty minutes,' Martindale said. 'That's where the good bit starts.'

Walker tutted once and pressed FORWARD. When the counter read twenty, he pressed PLAY.

>*Freddie, if we're wrong about Cairns we—*
>
>*We're not wrong. He said the loans letter was a definite fake, and your hunch about Merino . . .*

'That's Kate Hamilton and Fred Saunders, in case you hadn't recognised them,' Martindale said.

> *. . . it is the American base near Alice, and they're using it to spy on everyone.*

'Kate was a clever girl,' he remarked, as much to himself as to Walker.

'If you say so.'

'I do say so.'

'Is there much more of this diatribe? Walker's finger hovered above STOP.

'Keep listening, sport.'

> *She drives a bright red Mini, registration YZZ 997, and she will be at Julio's nightclub sometime after ten. Do you have the vial?*

'I expect you know who that is,' Martindale said.

Walker's face turned a mild shade of pink. He slapped his hand down and stopped the tape. 'Is there a point to all this?'

'You know damn well what the point is, you miserable piece of shit. That was you organising Kate's murder.'

'Oh, really?' Walker ejected the cassette.

'I'll have that back, Walker, or whatever your name really is.'

'You're welcome to it—it doesn't prove a thing.' He flung the cassette at Martindale as if it was a Frisbee.

Martindale snared it with one hand. 'There's enough on here to get you and your CIA cronies off my back. That much, I'm sure.'

'What do you intend doing with it?' Walker asked.

'Nothing, if you leave me and my son alone.'

'Otherwise?'

'Why worry if it doesn't prove anything?'

'May I remind you—'

'Otherwise, I guess I could always send it to Kate's editor. I'm sure he'd like it, especially the part where you're discussing her murder.'

'Don't be ridiculous, man.'

'It's on here, you fuck,' Martindale said, slipping the cassette into his breast pocket. 'Kate was investigating Merino, so you had her swatted away like a fly.'

'From memory, Professor, she was investigating you—your wife's untimely death, to be precise.'

Martindale paused before he came back with, 'She didn't have to die.'

'Who, your wife?'

'You really are a complete cunt, aren't you?'

'If you give that recording to the press,' Walker said, 'all you'll end up doing is exposing yourself.'

'I'm not sure I care anymore.'

'How about jail? Do you care about that?'

'That's probably where I belong,' Martindale answered.

Walker's jaw strained tighter than the guts of a golf ball.

'This,' Martindale said, giving a pat to his chest, 'will see you hanging from the highest tree, and that's all I'm interested in.'

'The only person swinging from a tree will be you. You were the one that killed your wife. I seem to recall you were happy enough for us to cover up that little fact.'

Martindale moulded his right hand into a fist so stiff it made his elbow crack.

'And *you* were the one that forged Cairns' signature,' Walker continued. '*You* sabotaged Connor, and *you* set up all the bogus loans. There is no evidence pointing to me, MI6 or the CIA.'

'It's your voice on the tape, not mine,' Martindale said. 'And Merino is real enough.'

'So what?'

'When the country finds out about it, they'll vote Whitlam back into power. Then you can kiss goodbye to that particular little secret.'

Walker returned a laugh that sprang deep from his belly. 'Is that what you think this is all about, that stupid base in the Outback?'

'That stupid base,' Martindale replied, 'was used to target bombs in Vietnam and fight a war Whitlam wanted no part of.'

'Oh, *pleeease*. Spare me the moralising bullshit. We were happy enough to help the Americans save Merino but only—'

'We being MI6?'

Walker sighed. 'Yes, if you like.'

'Do you ever give a straight answer?'

'I was trying to.'

Both men faced each other with their chests puffed like a pair of disgruntled baboons ready to fight for a prized female.

'Frankly, Mister Martindale, I couldn't care less about Merino. In any case, Whitlam is on record stating that he wasn't going to interfere with it.'

'Only because he didn't know it was run by the CIA.'

'Oh, what utter balls. Plenty of Australians work there as well.'

'Yeah, as cooks and cleaners.'

Walker shook his head. 'You don't have a clue why we needed Whitlam out of the way, do you? Neither did that girlfriend of yours.'

'Then why kill her?'

'I didn't.'

Martindale abruptly turned his head towards the hall. Did he hear something?

'What is it now?' Walker asked.

Keeping watch on Walker, Martindale stepped to the open door, his right arm tensed ready to grab the pistol at his back. He poked his head around the doorframe—there was nothing to see.

'I told you,' Walker said, 'no one else is in the house.'

Martindale let his arm relax. He moved back towards Walker, stopping a little closer to him than before. 'I wouldn't be too smug about what I do and do not know if I were you. A few weeks ago, a young lady by the name of Cathy Stansfield came to see me and—'

'How exciting for you.'

'Shut up and listen.'

Walker folded his arms and projected an air of smug boredom.

'Her husband, Tom,' Martindale continued, 'has been sent to prison for the next forty years.'

'That had nothing to do with me.'

'Really? She has a pretty good memory of you dragging him off in the middle of the night.'

'Just get on with it, Martindale. Say whatever it is you want to say, and leave.'

'You're right; I should get on with it.' He reached around his back and took hold of the pistol. With his elbow snug against his side to stop his hand from shaking, he aimed the barrel at Walker's chest.

'Now wait a minute,' Walker said, his arms unfolded and half-raised. 'What do you think you're doing?'

'Besides the tape, Cathy's husband had a few other goodies stashed away. This gun for starters, plus some very curious documents on uranium mining.'

Walker's breath came in a hard rasping gasp. 'I don't think—'

'*No*,' Martindale howled, 'you didn't think. You're lying about Kate, you son of a bitch. You killed her and I want to know why.'

He aimed the pistol at Walker's head. 'If this is not about Merino, then what the fuck is it all this about?'

'All right, I'll tell you. I tell you everything, but please put the gun down.'

Martindale's aim stayed true.

'You won't see me again, I promise.' A few globs of sweat sprouted across Walker's forehead. 'My work here is finished and I'm packed ready to leave—you saw the bags in the hall. You can do as you want now, and I assure you no harm will come to your son. He will be completely safe.'

'Like Kate was safe?'

'You're wrong about her,' Walker rushed. 'I know it sounds bad on that tape, but you have to let me explain. I'll tell you what happened, just *please* put the gun down.'

Martindale eased the pistol to his side. 'Now talk.'

'Thank you . . . I will.' With a peek at the drinks cabinet behind him, Walker asked, 'Would you like a whisky?'

'No.'

'Single malt.'

'*No.*'

'Do you mind if I have one?'

'It's your house.'

Walker turned.

'*Slowly,*' Martindale sounded. He stiffened his hold on the pistol but kept it pointing at the floor.

Walker stepped across to the cabinet and, with his back to Martindale, took a firm hold of the dark blue crystal decanter that adorned it. 'Tell me something, Professor, where was the tape hidden? I'm rather curious.'

'Just pour your whisky.'

191

Without removing the glass stopper, Walker rotated the decanter and extracted the snub-nosed revolver hidden in its thick base. Holding the decanter in front of him, masking the revolver in his right hand, he turned to face Martindale. 'Are you sure I can't tempt you with a drop?'

'All I want from you is to know why Kate was murdered.'

Walker returned an uncertain smile and, with the revolver pointed at Martindale's heart, lowered the decanter.

A single gunshot was followed by the thud of dead weight crashing to the floor.

35. The confession

It was probably the only time in his life Martindale had paid attention to another man's shoes, but the upward-pointing soles of Walker's Italian leather loafers poised in front of him were difficult to ignore. Heels together and toes apart, they formed an almost perfect V. Elegant. Polished. Unscuffed. And utterly motionless.

Had he shot Walker dead?

Was *he* shot? Crouched on the floor, ears ringing, stomach churning, Martindale fought his unwilling lungs for each scrap of air—air that stank of whisky, gunpowder and panic. He frisked his middle and chest for blood—there was none—and braced himself to stand.

'Don't move,' came a shout from the front window.

In one action, Martindale spun on his knees and took aim at the vague figure outside the window.

'Careful,' came another shout.

Martindale's entire body stiffened as Palmer's face came into view.

'Drop it, Professor.' Cradled in both hands, Palmer's nine millimetre Luger was directed at Martindale's head. '*Drop it.*'

Martindale placed his gun on the floor.

'Now slide it over here.'

He did so.

'Stay there.' Palmer slid the bottom half of the window fully up, eased himself through, seized Martindale's gun and tucked it into the front waistband of his denims. He moved across the room to where Walker lay beside the desk, and gave a gentle kick to his torso. There was no reaction. He gave another kick and then stooped to feel for a pulse in Walker's neck. Standing, with his Luger aimed loosely at Martindale's midsection, Palmer declared, 'He's dead.'

Martindale rose, bit by bit, his temples and scalp throbbing in unison with each heartbeat. 'Am I next?' he asked.

'That wasn't my intention,' Palmer replied with a voice calm and ordinary. He braced the toe of his left shoe against the side of the desk and put the Luger into an ankle holster. Foot down, jeans adjusted, his eyes made a swift survey of the room, ending at the blood oozing from Walker's chest. 'It was good shooting, Professor.'

Martindale's strained neck managed an uneasy nod. 'Kate said there was an agent in the House, but I never dreamed it could be you. I actually thought you were one of my better students.'

'Sorry to disappoint.'

'So what are you . . . CIA, NSA?'

'CIA.'

'Do I have you to thank for smashing my skull in?'

Palmer paused, taking in Martindale's words before he replied with, 'You didn't have a stroke?'

'Not yet, at least,' Martindale replied. 'What exactly did the CIA want you to do?'

Palmer paused again, his eyes darting upwards and to the right as if searching for a decent explanation. 'Langley was paranoid about Whitlam and wanted to know his every move. They figured

I might learn something if I was set up as your research student. Mostly, they wanted to know what he had planned for Merino.'

'Whitlam didn't have any plans for Merino. He thought it was a space research centre.'

'That's all I know,' Palmer said. 'What I didn't know is that you work for MI6.'

'I *don't* work for MI6.'

'That's not what it sounded like.' Palmer looked again at Walker's bloodied chest and said, 'How many teachers can shoot someone straight through the heart while diving to the floor?'

'I had my eyes closed, Geoff. It was the luckiest shot in the world.'

Palmer's mouth crimped shut.

'Believe me,' Martindale continued, 'I don't work for MI6 or any other agency.'

'Then why did you double-cross Cairns and Whitlam?'

'Because I had to,' came the blunt comeback.

'They were blackmailing you?'

'*He* was,' Martindale said with a cutting look to the body. 'Do you know him?'

'Not really. I saw him once at Merino.'

'You don't know anything about him?'

'I know he would have killed you had you not killed him first.'

Martindale considered the revolver in Walker's dead hand. 'What happens now?'

'You give me that cassette in your jacket and we leave.'

'No,' came the quick refusal. 'I can't do that, Geoff.'

'I'm trying to help, Professor. You don't understand how dangerous that recording is.'

'Sure I do, which is why I'm keeping it. It's my insurance and the best chance I have of and getting my life back.'

'That's never going to happen. Do you think Cathy Stansfield will ever get her life back?'

'How the hell do you know about—'

'I bugged your office.'

'Jesus . . . you really are something else.'

'I'm sorry about Missus Stansfield,' Palmer said. 'I'm sorry about everything, especially if it's true what you said about Kate Hamilton.'

'It is true, Geoff. That bastard rotting at your feet had her killed by one of your *compatriots*.' He spat out the final word as if it was the greatest insult.

'Which is exactly what they'll do to you if you keep hold of that tape,' Palmer replied. 'So, hand it over.'

Martindale stood firm.

Palmer moved forward and, with his right hand rested on the butt of the gun stuck in his jeans, held out his left hand. 'Please, Professor.'

With a full mask of defeat and a jaw tight enough to snap, Martindale handed the cassette to Palmer. 'What's to stop me from just giving the whole damn story to the press?'

'They'll crucify you, that's what. In less than a week, you will be branded a two-faced, low-life alcoholic.' With a nod to the corpse, Palmer added, 'And a murderer.'

Martindale eyed the pool of blood on the carpet, now ten inches wide and lapping at the near-empty whisky decanter lying on its side.

'The CIA will magic up evidence to paint you any way they want,' Palmer continued. 'More likely, though, you won't even get a chance to talk . . . if you get my drift.'

'I do.'

'Poisoning is their preferred method these days,' Palmer said. 'It could be in anything you eat, and likely served up by someone you know.'

'What should I do?'

'Was anyone else handling you besides Walker?'

'No.'

'Then go to work tomorrow, keep quiet and carry on as normal. You'll be all right.'

'Somehow, Geoff, I doubt that.'

A light shone through the open front window.

'Christ,' Martindale said, 'someone's coming.'

Palmer moved across to the window and peered out. The security lights were blazing but no one was about. He waited, listening for anything, but all he heard was the faint night clatter of the city's traffic. 'It must have been a fox or something.' He moved closer to the desk. 'Merino is secure, Professor, and I'm sure that's all the CIA was interested in.'

'Merino was nothing but a sideshow in all this crap,' Martindale replied. 'Walker was right—Whitlam had no plans to close the base. Something else is going on and I'm convinced uranium is the key to whatever it is.'

Palmer glanced to the front window as the garden went dark again.

'Those notes you gave me on the Nugan-Hand Bank,' Martindale said, 'were a crock of shit.'

'Tell me about uranium,' Palmer said.

'You tell me.'

Palmer returned a hesitant shrug.

'You're standing there, Geoff, with a dead MI6 officer at your feet like it's something that happens every day. Forgive me, but I find it hard to believe you don't know what else is going on.'

'I'm finding it hard to believe myself. Now I'm mixed up in all this rubbish, having to trail you about like I'm some sort of heartsick puppy.'

'Why didn't you let Walker shoot me, then? It might have been easier for everybody, including me.'

'Because I thought you were one of the good guys.'

'Yeah . . . me too, once.'

'How did they blackmail you?'

Martindale blew air through his lips. 'They knew my weakness for booze, and I guess they figured I'd screw up sooner or later. They figured right, of course, though I doubt they expected me to screw up in quite such a spectacular way.'

'Your wife?'

Martindale's whole body slumped into a bubble of insignificance.

'What happened?' Palmer asked.

'There's not a lot to tell,' Martindale replied, looking anywhere short of Palmer's gaze. 'I was drunk and crashed my boat into Coronation Bridge. Sarah died instantly, while I survived with nothing more than a cut cheek. Cops and security everywhere, and I remember seeing Walker in the crowd. Before I knew it, without being breathalyzed or even questioned, I was on my way home. The accident report made it look like the boat was faulty—it wasn't, of course. When Walker finally showed up at my door, he made it clear what the price of my freedom would be.'

'Sabotage the government?'

'Yes,' came the muffled reply. 'I refused at first, but then he threatened my son. Right away, I knew I was trapped.' Then, with a voice suddenly business-like, Martindale asked, 'What do I do about Walker?'

Palmer hunched his shoulders as though the question was an irrelevance. 'Nothing.'

'*Nothing*? It's not like the guy died of natural causes, Geoff. He's sprawled there covered in blood with a bullet in his heart.'

'I'm sure that particular detail won't appear in the news. Most likely, Walker's death won't be reported anywhere.' He wiped the edge of the desk with the cuff of his shirt. 'Did you touch anything?'

'What?'

'In this house, this room. Did you touch anything?'

'Oh . . . .' Martindale looked over the room. 'No, nothing.'

'Then go home now and don't come back here.'

'Am I going to see you again?'

Palmer stared at Martindale for a long moment before delivering his single-word response, 'No.'

Alone, Palmer made an unsuccessful attempt at opening the safe. He then searched each drawer of the desk but took nothing.

Wiping the drawers of fingerprints, his eyes were drawn to a photo frame sitting behind a cassette recorder. He used his handkerchief to pinch a corner of the frame and lay it face up on the desk. The faded image of a young newlywed couple standing in front of a chapel drew no reaction from him at first, but there was something about the bride's face that held his attention. He leaned in for a closer view. A moment later, his face went ash-grey.

36. No more screw-ups

Later that night

Mrs Henderson looked around her office as if viewing it for the first (or last) time, taking in every detail from floor to ceiling. Several seconds slipped away before the chimes of a distant clock broke her survey. It was ten p.m. She left at once, crossed the lobby to the prime minister's door and announced her entrance with two crisp knocks.

Whitlam looked up from his desk. 'June, you're an absolute marvel. Thank you for finishing all those letters.'

She tilted her head to one side and gave a warm smile.

'Where would I be without you?' Whitlam said.

'I am sure you would survive without me, Prime Minister.'

'Ahh, but I'm *not* the Prime Minister. Our dear friend down the road has seen to that.' He sat back. 'At least I have the office for a few more weeks.'

'If you don't mind me saying, I am sure the voters will tell *our friend* to take a flying leap.'

'I certainly do not mind, June. Let's hope you're right.'

She nodded—a nod of solidarity. 'I'm heading home unless you need anything else.'

'No, I'm done here. Margaret just phoned and ordered me to do the same.'

'Good for her.'

Whitlam's smile was broad and knowing. 'Good night, June.'

'Good night . . . Prime Minister.'

He nodded—a nod of appreciation.

*

The guard sitting by the exit stood up as Mrs Henderson approached.

'Goodnight, Jim,' she said.

'Another late night, Missus H.'

'It never ends, does it?' she replied.

'I suppose not.' The guard tipped his head goodnight and held the door open.

Once in the chilly air of the night, Mrs Henderson dipped inside her handbag for a cigarette. She moved to the edge of the top step, lit the cigarette and devoured it with a few hungry drags.

A set of headlights flashed in the far left corner of the car park.

She peeked behind—no one was about—flicked the butt away and descended the steps to the darkness beyond.

Commander Farnsworth was sitting in the driver's seat of a dark-coloured Ford LTD, bathed in the aftermath of his own nicotine habit.

Mrs Henderson walked in a beeline to him and said, 'Sorry I'm late.'

'Go around and get in,' he replied, exhaling a lungful of smoke out the window.

She did so.

He wound the window up, stubbed his rollup in the ashtray, grumbled something under his breath and then stated, with finality, '*Pineapples* is back on.'

Mrs Henderson threw a sideways stare at him. 'But the Governor-General has—'

'The Aussies are going ape-shit about Whitlam being sacked by that sleazeball. I warned MI6 this would happen.'

'Whitlam's gone, isn't he?' Mrs Henderson offered. 'Langley should be happy for that.'

'Gone for how long?' Farnsworth snapped. 'If we don't do anything, he'll be voted back into office next month. A permanent solution was needed from the start, not this airy-fairy bullshit with Kerr.'

Her back stiffened a little and she rose in her seat.

At that moment, a light-haired man driving a Mercedes Benz pulled alongside them. It was Scott Williams.

'What is *he* doing here?' Mrs Henderson asked, her face streaked with dread.

'He's here because I told him to be here,' Farnsworth replied.

With a cake tin tucked under his left arm, Williams climbed out of the Mercedes and got into the back seat of the Ford, behind Mrs Henderson. He passed the tin to Farnsworth without saying a word.

Farnsworth pressed the ceiling light and popped the lid of the tin. No sooner had he done so, the car filled with a scent of chocolate. 'So that's what a lamington looks like.' He faced Williams. 'They smell nice, at least. You baked these yourself?'

Williams bore a smile of pure pride. 'Yep.'

Mrs Henderson leaned over and peeked at the cakes. She scowled at Farnsworth and said, 'You don't seriously think I'm going to give these to Whitlam, do you?'

'I do, and you will.' Farnsworth replaced the lid, turned the light off and held the cake tin out for her to take.

She bolted her arms across her chest and said, with words clipped and certain, 'No, I will not. Langley would never have sanctioned this. It is preposterous *and* unnecessary. Walker has succeeded in—'

'Walker's dead,' Williams said with a face showing all the emotion of an unbaked bread roll.

For a second or two, neither Farnsworth nor Mrs Henderson made any sound whatsoever. Then, Farnsworth turned in his seat and asked, 'What did you say?'

Williams dragged an errant lock of hair off the right side of his face, looped it around his ear and repeated, in the same flat voice, 'Walker's dead.'

Mrs Henderson sucked in her upper lip, bit down hard and turned her head away.

'Martindale shot him,' Williams explained.

'Martindale?' Farnsworth said. 'He's out of the hospital?'

'Seems so.'

'*Jesus H Christ!* What in the name of Sam Hill happened?'

After another hair adjustment, Williams replied, 'Martindale tailed Walker home from the Governor-General's and—'

'He saw Kerr?' Farnsworth interrupted.

'Nope, I don't think so. The kid followed Martindale and I followed the kid.' He chuckled, adding, 'It was like a hometown parade on the fourth of July out there.'

'Get on with it, Williams.'

'I slipped into the house around the back and saw the whole thing through the kitchen hatch. Martindale was armed and had that tape you've been looking for, and he was trying to blackmail Walker with it. But Walker sure wasn't about to let that happen, and pulled a gun on him. Martindale was too nifty, though. He crashed to the floor, took aim and hit Walker through the heart from about fifteen feet away.' Williams stopped and snorted a laugh. 'Pretty neat shooting for a professor.'

Mrs Henderson scowled at Williams, her eyes colder than a northern gale.

'Where was Palmer in all this?' Farnsworth said to Williams.

'Standing outside the front window. He climbed in after the shooting and persuaded Martindale to give him the cassette. I left soon after.'

'Then you had better pay Palmer a visit,' Farnsworth said.

'What about Martindale?' Williams asked.

'We'll deal with him later.'

'Are you sure we can wait? Martindale will be at work tomorrow if he follows Palmer's advice.'

Mrs Henderson rose in her seat.

'Martindale would have been rotting in the ground by now if you'd done your job properly,' Farnsworth said. 'I *don't* want any more screw-ups, Williams. Now go and clear up the mess at Walker's house, then find Palmer. Do whatever it is you have to do, but don't come back without that tape.'

Williams opened the car door to leave.

'And one more thing,' said Farnsworth.

Williams stopped.

'Get a haircut.'

In silence, both Farnsworth and Mrs Henderson watched Williams drive away, losing sight of him at the highway turning.

'Now see here, June,' Farnsworth said with stiff politeness. 'Langley *did* approve the plan. Hell, it was their idea. All you have to do—'

She snatched the lamingtons from Farnworth's hands. 'I know what I have to do.' Her voice held no hint of unease. 'These better work the way you hope they do.'

'The poison will induce a fatal heart attack in minutes,' Farnsworth said. 'It's supposed to be untraceable in the body, but be sure to remove any half-eaten cakes before raising the alarm.' With modest conviction, he concluded with, 'It might be best not to lick your fingers.'

37. The detour

11.45 am, the following day

Sat on the edge of the bed, Palmer stared at his rucksack that lay slumped against the wall opposite. It contained everything he held precious—Nikon camera and a few glossy prints—some cash, a change of clothes and toiletries. It also contained a fresh passport with his face above someone else's name, airline tickets in that same name, plus directions to a safe house in the outer suburbs of Auckland, New Zealand.

There was a polite knock at the door.

Palmer stood. 'Come in.'

Viktor Dobrogorskiy entered—unsteady, even with his cane—and closed the door behind him. He scanned the rucksack before giving a look to Palmer that was half pity and half guilt. 'It is most unfortunate that—' He stopped as a brutal, racking cough erupted.

Palmer winced. 'Are you all right?' he asked reflexively, but in a way that signalled genuine concern.

Dobrogorskiy either didn't hear the question or chose to ignore it. He rooted out a silver hip flask from the inside of his coat, took two swift sips and looked again at the totality of Palmer's belongings. 'I am sorry you were not able to retrieve all your possessions. We will do our best to deliver them to you in a short while.'

'You needn't bother, I took everything I wanted.' He checked his watch. 'I better get going. I've made up my mind to see Farnsworth, then I'll go to the airport.'

The old man's face fell into an uneasy scowl as he returned the flask to its hiding place. 'You do not have to do this?' His voice was soft but urgent.

'Yes, I do. The only way to deal with Farnsworth is to threaten him. He needs to know the tape will go public if he makes a move against Whitlam.'

With a lingering gaze at the door, Dobrogorskiy answered, 'Yes, but—'

'But, what? You said it would guarantee Whitlam's safety.'

'It is not Mister Whitlam I am concerned about. For your own protection, you should keep to our arrangement and go without delay to the airfield.'

'They're not going to do anything to me.'

'Please hear what I have to say. You have done the right thing by bringing the tape recording to us. Now you must disappear for some time at least. Understand, they will never let you be free.'

'I'll be all right as long as—'

'You *must* listen to me.'

'All I'm going to—'

'*Listen to me, Pavel!*' Dobrogorskiy snapped, striking his cane hard against the floor.

Palmer rocked back on his heels.

The old man gave a world-weary sigh, lifted a hand and smoothed his temple with tightknit fingers. He whispered something to himself before looking Palmer in the eye. 'I apologise, Mister Palmer.'

'You don't need too,' Palmer replied, sounding as uneasy as he looked. 'Maybe it's best if I—'

'Pavel was my son. You remind me of him very much. Like you, he was strong-willed and full of passion.'

Palmer felt his cheeks warm.

'Mister Palmer . . . .' Dobrogorskiy stopped and then began again. 'Geoffrey . . . you are young and in a hurry to change the way things are. I understand this. But you must recognize that Farnsworth is not to be trusted. Few people in this profession can be trusted, and that includes my comrades here at the embassy.' He coughed once more, leaning heavily on his walking stick. Was all his strength gone?

'I have to put things right,' Palmer said. 'At the very least, I want to make sure Whitlam will be safe. If Farnsworth knows—'

Dobrogorskiy held up his hand to Palmer. 'Please, Geoffrey, indulge me this one last time.' The heartfelt plea in his scratchy voice was inescapable.

'Sorry.' Palmer's apology was more in recognition of the old man's failing health than for anything else.

'A back channel can be used,' Dobrogorskiy continued, 'to inform the CIA we have incriminating evidence against them. This is the best option.'

Palmer stood firm. Was this a genuine offer or was he being played for a fool by both the CIA *and* the KGB? 'Forgive me for asking, but why do you care what happens to me? I'm grateful, of course, but . . . why?'

Dobrogorskiy paused before revealing, 'When Pavel needed me the most, I was not there for him. I failed him, and it cost him his life.'

Unsure of how to respond to the old man's torn soul, Palmer said nothing.

'Being here carries a great risk for you, Geoffrey. That was my doing and it is up to me to protect you, which is what I am trying to do. You must leave Australia today.'

'I intend to.'

'Let me take you to the airfield now.'

Palmer's lips levelled in a hard, unbent line. He took a breath through his nose and held it for a hesitant second before exhaling. 'I understand, but I'd prefer to go to the airport by myself. Anyway, it seems to me you need to rest.'

'Yes, you are correct. My age has some benefits but stamina is not one of them.'

Palmer's face softened.

'When you arrive at the airfield,' Dobrogorskiy said, 'you must go through immigration immediately. Only then, will you be safe.'

'I will, don't worry.'

Dobrogorskiy gave a protective squeeze to Palmer's upper arm. 'I made the reservation myself. No one here knows you are flying out tonight, and no one except myself knows about the safe house in New Zealand. Once you are there, you will be secure.'

'Thank you . . . for everything.'

'You are very welcome, my boy.'

'Is there a phone I could use to order a taxi?'

Dobrogorskiy shook his head. 'Not from here. Use the payphone on the corner of Lockyer and Gregory. It is only one block east.'

'You don't trust your own Embassy staff?'

'In this profession, Geoffrey, it is wise not to trust anybody.' Dobrogorskiy gave a paternal smile and continued, 'As an old man, may I offer you one more piece of advice?'

'Sure.'

'Seek a different profession. You do not belong in this one.'

Palmer's toothy grin was wiped clean by a string of chimes. 'Lunch?' he quizzed.

'Yes. Soon, everyone will be in the dining room. This is good. I will show you a way out to avoid our spirited guards.'

*

Palmer set his bag face up on the back seat of the taxi and checked the contents of its front compartment. With a satisfied sigh, he sat back and said, 'Could you make a right at the next intersection?'

'The airport's straight on, mate.'

'I'm not going to the airport.'

'Make up your mind.'

'Do you know the American Diner on Amaroo Street?' Palmer asked.

'Yes.'

'Drop me there.'

38. Jabiluka

12.40 pm

Palmer relaxed a little when he saw that the diner was three-quarters full with the lunchtime crowd. He spotted Farnsworth sitting alone in a corner booth, reading—or at least pretending to read—the menu. He walked up to the booth and slung his bag onto the empty bench seat.

Farnsworth's welcoming smile held all the charm of a rush-hour commuter train into Sydney. 'What are the pancakes like here?' he asked.

Palmer slid next to his bag. 'I didn't know we'd be eating.'

'You chose the place, not me.'

'I chose it because I knew it would be busy.'

Farnsworth browsed the neighbouring tables. 'Yep, sure is.' Returning his gaze, he produced a warmer smile. 'It's good that you called us, son. We were beginning to think something happened to you.'

'Is that so?'

'Where have you been?'

'With friends.'

'Friends, eh? That's nice.' Farnsworth went back to the menu. 'Should I have the pancakes or the hamburger with fries?'

Palmer stared at the spidery veins that crisscrossed Farnsworth's nose, and the rolls of fat around his neck. He dryly offered, 'Why not have both?'

Farnsworth sat back, looked Palmer dead in the eye and said, in a voice no greater than a whisper, 'What to do with you?'

'Sorry, what?'

'Did you bring the tape?' Farnsworth asked.

After a pointed delay, Palmer leaned out of the booth and checked that no one was standing close. Sitting easily again, he pronounced, 'George Martindale's out of hospital.'

'So I heard.'

'According to the papers, he had a stroke.'

Farnsworth's mouth twisted up in one corner.

'What really happened to him?' Palmer asked.

'Where's the tape, son?'

'And what happened to Kate Hamilton,' Palmer went on, 'her parents and Fred Saunders?'

There was no reply.

'You can add Walker to that list, by the way.'

'*Yes*, Walker,' Farnsworth replied, biting off his words. 'Perhaps you could tell me about him?'

Until that moment, Palmer was uncertain if anyone had tailed him to Walker's house. Now he knew. He reached into the front compartment of his rucksack and fished out a photograph, deliberately playing for time as he had yet to decide on his next move. He glided the photo across the table with the tips of his fingers and said, 'I found this on Walker's desk.'

Farnsworth did not touch the photo, and only considered it for the briefest moment. 'I'm not interested in wedding memorabilia.'

'You should be. The young bride in the picture is Missus Henderson . . . and she's standing next to Walker.'

Farnsworth's brows snapped together. He leant forward, lifted the print with his left hand and squinted hard at it. '*Jeeesus*.' The knuckles of his right hand popped as his fingers coiled into a fist.

'Was she MI6 as well?' Palmer asked.

'You'll know as soon as we do.' Farnsworth took a breath and released it as a grumbling sigh. 'Let's move on, son.' His manner was suddenly calm, almost cordial. He handed the photograph back. 'You said you had the tape for us. That's great work, Palmer.'

Palmer felt as though his windpipe had sealed over. The gentle tones he was now hearing were far more frightening than the various tongue-lashings he had received in the past. 'What I want—'

'How about passing it over now?' Farnsworth's cheesy grin bared a full set of yellow teeth.

'Later,' Palmer said. 'First, there are some things we need to discuss.'

Farnsworth scanned the diner. 'Where the hell is the waiter?'

Shelving his growing irritation, Palmer replied calmly, 'You order at the counter.'

'Don't they even bring coffee?'

'You won't get away with it,' Palmer stated.

'I won't get away with what?'

'Knocking off Whitlam.'

'Christ, Palmer, keep it down.'

'I know what all this is about,' Palmer said.

'Do tell.'

'Money.'

'Been snooping around Nugan-Hand, have we?'

'Yes, I have,' Palmer replied. 'For a bank, it sure has a very curious list of personnel. By my reckoning, there are probably enough military men and spooks on staff to run a small war.'

'What you don't—'

'But I'm not talking about Nugan-Hand.'

'Let's not drag this out, son. What prize bit of intel do you have?'

'Nabarlek and Koongarra.'

The names were met with stony silence.

'And Jabiluka,' Palmer added. 'Great name for a town, isn't it? I wonder what it's like to live there.'

'Your point is what?' Farnsworth's voice signalled disinterest but his eyes were lively.

'Those towns have the largest deposits of uranium in the world, worth billions,' Palmer said. 'And that's it, isn't it? This whole stupid operation was about uranium, who has it and who controls it.'

'Where are you getting this?'

'*Wasn't it?*'

Farnsworth took a moment to adjust his posture and said, 'You know, I think I'll have the pancakes.'

'Answer me, damn you!' Palmer could feel himself wound tighter than a hangman's noose.

'Yes, all right, it was,' Farnsworth replied. 'It still is.'

His voice low and guarded, like a parent scolding a child in a community library, Palmer said, 'How could you destroy one of our closest allies just to let a few American mining companies make more money?'

'It's not quite that simple, son. You don't seem to understand—'

'The only thing I don't understand is why I signed up to this outfit in the first place. But at least that's one decision I can do something about.'

'What you need to do, Palmer, is get off that high horse of yours and accept a few hard facts.' Farnsworth cocked his head. 'Where are you getting this information?'

'Does it matter?'

'It might.'

'I didn't bring the tape with me,' Palmer announced with a burst. He paused, waiting for Farnsworth's veins to pop, eyes to bulge. But all he got was a deadpan shrug, so he went on, 'I left it with my friends. I only came here to warn you that if Whitlam goes down, my friends will make that tape public.'

'You shouldn't have done that, son.' Farnsworth had the air of a judge about to condemn a man to death, his face drained of warmth or pity. 'We're not going to touch Whitlam now. Things have moved on since we last spoke, and it is plain to see that Malcolm Fraser has this election in the bag.' He put a hand under the lapel of his coat and appeared to press something. 'You haven't understood anything, have you?'

'Want a bet?'

'Come on, let's go,' Farnsworth said.

'*Wait*. That tape is also my insurance.'

Farnsworth pulled himself out of the booth and stood over Palmer.

Looking up, Palmer continued, 'If I happen to slip on a banana skin and crack my head open or—'

'Yeah, I get it. Now grab your bag and come with me.' Farnsworth walked away.

Against every crumb of good sense, against every instinct to either stay put or run as fast he could, Palmer trailed Farnsworth out of the restaurant.

39. Hell

1.05 pm

Martindale sat in his car with the engine running, staring at the entrance to Parliament House as though it was a portal to hell. In his mind, he could see Walker's distorted grey face and bloodied chest, a memory that both pleased and terrified him. Was he finally free, or would it only be a matter of time before he was chained to another devil?

He forced the image of Walker from his mind, only for the torment of Kate's red Mini clinging for air in Lake Burley Griffin to replace it. The pit of his stomach grew cold as his emotions lurched from anger to fear, and back again.

Could he carry on as Palmer suggested and act like nothing had happened? A dozen scenarios crowded his head before he settled on one: work through the next few weeks, resign after the election and leave politics forever. His teaching post was still open to him. He could give up the booze. If Tim was by his side, he could do anything. The days to come would be difficult, but then his nightmare charade would be over.

After popping an antacid tablet to calm his rolling gut, he set off for hell.

*

With an empty stomach and a head full of whiskey, Martindale breathed shallow to curb the suffocating stink of wood panelling in the Prime Minister's lobby. He stopped by Mrs Henderson's fully open door and said, 'Hello, June.' They were the first words he had uttered that day, and his voice was croaky.

She stopped typing and looked up, her face displaying all the warmth of a grizzly bear. She said nothing.

Martindale was not expecting her to throw any wild parties on his return from oblivion, but he was expecting a smile, perhaps even a warm embrace. 'Is everything all right, June?'

'The hospital telephoned to say to say you might be coming in today. They sounded quite worried about you.'

'I'm fine.'

'You don't look it.'

'You don't look too happy yourself, June. Is something wrong?'

'No.' Her puffy eyes said otherwise. 'You know what's happened, of course?' She glanced over his shoulder to Whitlam's door.

'Yes. Gough still has the PM's office?'

'For the moment.'

'Is he in?'

'No.'

'Well . . . doesn't matter. I didn't want to stay long today. I'll catch up with him later in the week.'

'I'll be sure to tell him.' Her offer reeked of indifference.

Martindale walked up to her desk. 'Are you sure you're okay, June? Because you seem—'

'I sorted your post.'

He paused, unsure of what to say or how to say it. 'That's great,' he said finally. 'Thank you.'

'I have dealt with most of it. Everything else is on your desk.'

'I guess there's a mountain of it.' He used a breezier air, hoping to break the tension flung his way. 'I'll try to read through as much—'

'I made a few lamingtons for you as well.' She leaned down and opened the oversized bottom drawer of her desk, extracted a cake tin and, along with an unsteady smile, gave it to Martindale.

He smiled back. 'You're a star, June, as always.'

'They are for you,' she said in a way that sounded more like a command than an act of kindness. With that, her smile disappeared and she went back to her work.

'Thanks again.' He wanted to say more but nothing seemed appropriate. He turned and left for his office.

40. The double-cross

1.10 pm

Standing with Farnsworth on the pavement in front of the diner, Palmer did not register the grey-suited man leaning on a gum tree in the park opposite.

Farnsworth rolled a cigarette between his stubby fingers, lit it and took a long drag. 'You only had one job to do, Palmer.' He spat out a scrap of tobacco and continued, 'You should have trusted us and followed your orders. Everything we're doing is in the best interests of our country and world security.' He took another drag.

'I'd hardly call plotting to murder the leader of a sovereign state the best option for world security.'

'Listen up, son,' Farnsworth cracked. 'Not only is there a cosy little cartel operating here, driving the price of uranium through the roof, Whitlam and his cronies are in bed with the Japs to build an enrichment plant. A setup like that could destroy our control of nuclear programmes around the world, civilian *and* military. Do you understand what I'm saying?'

'Sure . . . the world's only safe if we're in charge.'

'Grow up, Palmer, and take a look around. Would you rather some mad dictator from Korea was in control? There are dozens of little despots scattered around the world. How safe do you think we'd be if any one of them got their hands on a nuclear weapon?'

'That doesn't justify—'

'And down the line,' Farnsworth went on, 'we're going to need nuclear power to run our industries. We can't rely on oil forever, not with those fucking Arabs have ninety percent of it.'

'All Whitlam was trying to do was develop Australia's own energy supplies?' Palmer replied.

'Haven't you understood a word I've said? *We* need to keep control of uranium. It's that simple.'

'You mean *we* need to keep control of the profits.'

Farnsworth took a final drag and, blowing the smoke skywards, flicked the glowing rollup into the gutter. 'I guess you'd prefer the Russians were in control?'

A deep-seated burning travelled the length of Palmer's spine and jumped to his knees. 'So,' he said, fighting for a confident voice, 'you know who my friends are?'

'Yes.'

'Why am I not surprised?' But Palmer was surprised, and the old man's warning that Farnsworth couldn't be trusted suddenly echoed in his head. 'Tell me something . . . .' He took a step away. 'Why is MI6 involved?'

'Because Whitlam wanted everything—uranium, oil, gas, coal. And that apparently upset some fat cats back in England.'

'Who?'

'You'll have to ask MI6,' Farnsworth replied, glancing over Palmer's shoulder.

Palmer swivelled around and saw a familiar dark-coloured agency car approaching. Turning back, he spotted the suited agent from the park crossing the road. A second agent, dressed in the same grey garb, emerged from the diner.

'Better still,' Farnsworth said with a snap in his voice, 'why not raise it at your trial?'

The car stopped in a small lay-by beside them. A third agent bounded from the rear door. Seconds later, Palmer was surrounded. With the eyes of an injured foal, he faced Farnsworth and said, 'I wasn't bluffing about the tape.'

'What, this one?' Farnsworth said, producing a white cassette seemingly from thin air.

The lettering printed in felt pen on the side of the cassette ripped at Palmer's throat; fear and confusion hooked all his senses. He moved back, only to have his left arm hijacked. He felt a sharp pain in his ribs. Was it a gun?

'Look familiar, does it?' Farnsworth said with a menacing chuckle. 'You see, Palmer, I have friends too . . . in all sorts of places.'

'You can't do this.'

'We can do anything we damn well like. And that includes knocking off Whitlam.'

The agents standing before Palmer were both potbellied, and he could hear the wheezing of the man behind him. Could he risk trying to run for it? There was no doubt in his mind he could outrun all of them, but could he dodge a bullet? Before any ideas came, he was bundled into the open rear door of the car. The agent wielding a gun scooped Palmer's luggage from the pavement and scrambled into the car after him.

Farnsworth got into the front passenger seat and turned enough to face Palmer.

The driver took a sly peek in the rear-view. He kept the engine running.

'You're insane if you go through with this,' Palmer said. His skin from collar to jaw was blotchy red, his voice a pinch too loud.

'Calm down, son. We're not going to shoot you. Not here, at least.'

'If you think—'

'Shut up and listen, Palmer. You have a simple choice to make. Either you're with us or you're not. If you're with us, we can forget your little adventures over the past week. If you're not, we'll have you tried for treason and sent to prison for forty years.' He gave a self-satisfied smirk and added, 'Or . . . you could try and make a run for it.' He laughed at his own dead humour. The driver laughed with him.

Palmer looked at the agent by his side and the silver barrel pointed at his gut. Why didn't he follow the old man's advice and go directly to the airport? He needed to hold fast for a little longer. Raising his head to Farnsworth in a show of defiance, he said, slowly, 'You really are a dumb son-of-a-bitch.'

The smirk on Farnsworth's face evaporated.

'Did you think,' Palmer said, his heart thumping out of his chest, 'I would hand over the original tape to the Russians without making a copy for myself? I want out, *period*. Out of this car and out of the CIA. Otherwise, you and your cronies are finished.'

Looking at the agent in the backseat, Farnsworth cocked his head to one side.

With the snarl of a dog protecting its bone, the agent poked the barrel of his gun into Palmer's midsection.

'I'm not kidding,' Palmer said.

'Okay, son, I'll play along with your little game. Where is this duplicate tape, then?'

'With someone you'll never find.' His voice was a notch stronger. 'And they have clear-cut instructions on what to do with it.'

'Bullshit!' Farnsworth replied. 'You never made a copy.'

'Believe what you like.'

'What I believe is that you're lying through your teeth.' After a moment of eye-to-eye standoff, Farnsworth casually removed a packet of tobacco from his coat only to put it back again. 'All right, Palmer,' he said, 'have it your way.' He motioned for the agent to stow his gun. 'You can take a walk, but for how long, eh? How long before you get tired of looking over your shoulder?'

Palmer raised his right hand and wrapped his fingers around the door latch. 'If you want to take the risk, go right ahead. It'll be your funeral as well as mine.' He pulled on the latch, though not enough for the door to open.

'I bet you'd make one hell of a poker player, son.'

'It's your call.'

'Don't get smart with me, Palmer, or I'll shoot you myself right here and now just for the sheer fun of it.'

'Sorry,' Palmer said in a voice bordering on contempt.

'The likes of you or Martindale,' Farnsworth went on, 'will never succeed against us. That's how it is—the CIA always wins. We win because we know everything, we keep everything and we forget nothing.' Farnsworth glanced down at Palmer's fingers on the door latch. 'Go on, then, get the hell out of here before I change my mind.'

In quick fashion, Palmer grabbed his bag from the floor of the car and pushed the door open. Would death come quickly with one clean shot in his back? He rolled out of the car onto the edge of the road. There was no screaming bullet; no shouts for him to stop. Maybe his bluff was going to work. He slammed the door.

Freedom was a taxi ride away.

41. Tormented regret

1.20 pm

The lamingtons were not Mrs Henderson's usual hearty size, and Martindale swallowed the first one whole. The chocolate sauce was also different, though he couldn't pinpoint how exactly. He ate another.

Eyeing the third and last lamington, his stomach fluttered. Maybe three on the go would be one too many? He pushed the cake tin to one side, took a bunch of letters from the full "in" tray and started reading.

Five minutes went by.

The intercom buzzed—it was Mrs Henderson.

He pushed the speaker button. 'Yes, June?'

'Have you tried the lamingtons yet?'

'Yes, delicious as always. Just one left.'

'Good.'

'And thanks again for sorting my mail.' His mouth was dry, his tongue sticking to his teeth. 'I should finish most of it before I leave.' He gave a voiceless cry as the fluttering in his stomach mutated into a run of minor somersaults, kicking the back of his throat with a teaspoon of bile. He screwed up his face at the taste of the bitter residue.

The intercom stayed silent.

He swallowed hard and said, 'Was there something you wanted?'

'I gather you're an excellent marksman.'

He gawped at the intercom. Had he misheard her? He reached to turn the volume up, but his hand jerked back as a burning agony burst across his ribs. Holding his breath, he squeezed the flesh of his chest, digging his fingers in as hard as he could. A moment passed in stillness before the pain subsided. 'Sorry, June, I thought I was having a coronary there for a second. What did you say before?'

'Hitting his heart at fifteen feet while diving to the floor—quite impressive.'

He rose in his seat. What was he hearing? He drew a leaden breath past a growing tightness in his rib cage.

'My husband had clearly underestimated you.'

'What are you talking . . . .' He stopped as the tightness spread to his neck and jaw, and down his left arm.

'It shouldn't take too long,' Mrs Henderson said. Her tone was casual, as if hearing someone's cries of pain was something ordinary.

He held his arm rigid against his body. His eyes were dark, his mouth open.

'If you ate the last cake as well,' she added, 'it might speed things up a little.'

His eyes darted to the remaining lamington. 'Oh, Jesus, no . . .' he said, his voice a flat growl. The walls and ceiling seemed to sway and press down on him. Doubled over in torture, his right cheek mashed against the desk, he reached out with both hands, sending the 'in' tray and cake tin screaming to the floor.

'Goodbye, George.'

He pushed on the desk to stand, his face crimson red and bloated with agony and anger. In one convulsive movement, he gripped the intercom, yanked it free from cables and hurled it across the room before tumbling to the carpet like a rag doll. 'Tim . . . .' he said with a voice of tormented regret.

A column of light streamed in through the window and across the floor, stopping just shy of his outstretched hand.

42. The last crossing

Four weeks later, Friday 12 December 1975, California

The white-painted church with its shingled spire was located at the far edge of town, bounded by open fields to the north and a winding brook to the west. A morning mist hovered over the brook, but elsewhere the sky was clear. The winter sun gave a pleasant warmth to the day. A modest breeze carried the festive scents of pine and wood-burning fires. In the distance somewhere, the urgent chirps of a few sparrows cut through the trees.

A middle-aged couple stood alone in the church forecourt. Unmoved by the warmth of the sun or the scent of Christmas, they waited for their son to arrive. Long minutes passed. They did not move. They did not speak.

The morning's calm ended as a hearse turned into the grounds and stopped in front of the couple. It was their first sight of the coffin, and they both wept without restraint.

A priest emerged from the vestibule and stood beside them. Together, they watched as the coffin, adorned with ribbons of blue silk and a wreath of white lilies, was eased out of the car by the pallbearers and carried with measured steps through the archway.

Trailing behind, the mother kept her head down and did not look at the coffin. The father could not take his eyes off it.

The congregation of family and friends were waiting inside the church, some silent, some talking in whispers, some crying. They all fell quiet as the pallbearers glided the mahogany box down the aisle and laid it to rest on two decorative trestles near the foot of the altar.

The bearers walked back the length of the aisle and sat together in the rear pew. The priest took his place in the pulpit. The parents sat beside the coffin in the front pew. The father, ashen-faced and trembling, held his tears in check. The mother's tears were unrelenting.

Pachelbel's Canon floated above the sounds of crying, shuffling feet and creaking seats.

The service lasted one hour.

The bearers performed their duty in reverse and then, row by row, the church emptied. The parents were the last to leave.

An elderly man wearing a pinstriped suit with wide lapels and hard-pressed pleats was sitting by himself on a bench in the vestibule, a wooden cane by his side. His face was gaunt; a patchy wet sheen streaked his cheeks. The congregation walked right by him to the forecourt, with some members dispensing a furtive leer or muted comment. Only the parents stopped.

'May I help you?' the father said.

The old man answered, his voice croaky, 'I am all right, thank you.' He pulled a large white handkerchief from his coat and wiped his cheeks.

Taking her husband's hand, the mother asked, 'Did you know our son?'

The old man pressed down on the walking stick and stood. 'A little,' he said softly. 'Forgive me, I did not mean to intrude on your grieving.' His English was near faultless, but a foreign accent was unmistakable. He stepped towards the forecourt.

'Don't go,' the mother said. 'How did you know him?' Her tone was more interrogation than conversation.

Without quite meeting her eyes, he replied, 'I was on a sabbatical at the university in Canberra, and Geoffrey would sometimes consult me about his thesis.'

'And where is *your* university?' the father asked.

'Moscow.'

'Is that a fact?' came the father's cold return. 'Did you know Geoff's supervisor, George Martindale?'

The old man sidestepped the question. 'Your son was a fine young man, Mister and Missus Palmer. I am sorry for your loss.'

The father gave an appreciative smile. 'Thank you, Mister . . . .'

'Dobrogorskiy, Viktor Dobrogorskiy.'

As they shook hands, the father glanced outside. The coffin was back in the hearse, its full length visible through the car's oversized windows. 'Tell me something, Mister Dobrogorskiy. How did you know where Geoff's funeral would be?'

Dobrogorskiy hesitated a moment, but his face gave nothing away. 'It was reported in the university news.'

'And you flew all the way from Australia to be here?' said the mother.

'My work in Canberra was finished. I stopped here on my way home.'

The father shook his head and said, with the confidence of someone stating a fact, 'You people have an answer for everything.' He pulled a hand-written note from inside his jacket and held it out.

'Maybe you could explain why Geoff was writing to us on stationery from the Russian Embassy?'

Dobrogorskiy took the note and read it from start to finish in a slow, methodical manner. He handed it back without comment.

'Geoff was clearly unhappy with his work in Australia,' the father said. 'And you understand, I *don't* mean his thesis.'

Unblinking, with his mouth open, Dobrogorskiy looked poised to speak. But no words came.

'Our son wrote this note on Embassy paper for a reason, Mister Dobrogorskiy,' the father continued. 'Were you involved or not?'

'Yes.' The acknowledgement was soft but immediate.

'We understand who Geoff really worked for,' the mother said. 'If you know how he died, please tell us what happened. No matter how bad it is, we need to know.'

The song of footsteps on loose stones echoed in the quiet of the vestibule. Dobrogorskiy turned his head to the forecourt, where a small party from the congregation were milling around the hearse.

'They can't hear us,' the father said.

Dobrogorskiy gave a token nod. 'You must understand that Geoffrey had a valid reason for acting against the wishes of his employer.'

'We always had faith in whatever our son did,' the mother replied.

'Yes, I am sure,' Dobrogorskiy said. He gave another glance to the forecourt before continuing. 'I had planned every small detail of Geoffrey's escape, which included escorting him to the airfield. Unfortunately, Geoffrey did not appreciate the danger he was in, and insisted on travelling to the airfield by himself. On the way, he stopped and met with his senior officer—he was not aware that I followed him in my own car.'

The mother tightened her grip on her husband's hand.

'I was on my own, please realize, and there was little I could do to help.' Dobrogorskiy brought his hand up to his temple and pushed on it with pointed fingers as though quashing an ache.

'Oh, sweet Jesus,' the father said. 'They killed him?'

His hand down by his side again, the old man said, 'They may have wanted him dead, Mister Palmer, to tidy up their affairs, but . . . .'

'But, what?'

Dobrogorskiy's mind drifted back to the way his day had started, with a vision of Palmer's last moments. 'I saw Geoffrey walk out of a café with the officer. They talked for a small time on the sidewalk before other agents arrived in a car and forced Geoffrey into it. He got out of the car soon after, unharmed. Then . . . .'

The mother held still as she pleaded, 'Go on.'

Dobrogorskiy's lower jaw quivered as he bathed in her dread. 'At that moment, a taxi stopped on the opposite side of the road. I knew Geoffrey needed transport to the airfield and called to him, but my voice was not strong enough. Geoffrey raised his hand to the taxi and stepped out onto the road. But in his rush or confusion, he looked to the left.'

The father squinted. 'What are you telling us?'

'I recognise this is difficult for you to accept, Mister Palmer, but Geoffrey did not see the car coming. His death was an accident.'

The father responded, as much to himself as to the old man, 'Geoff died because he looked the wrong way crossing the road? Is *that* what you're asking us to believe?'

'That is what happened, yes.'

'What about the person who hit him?' the mother asked. 'Are you sure it wasn't a setup?'

'I am sure. The driver stopped and tried to help Geoffrey. Also, I made enquiries to be certain she was not connected to any Intelligence agencies, including my own.'

The mother's tears slipped to the flagstone floor, enough of them to form a small puddle at her feet. She sniffed back the fluid creeping from her nose and said, quietly, 'Thank you for telling us, Mister Dobrogorskiy.' She sniffed again, shaking her head. 'I don't understand why Geoff didn't take the chance you gave him. Why did he risk so much to meet with this officer again?'

'Because, Misses Palmer, he was trying to put things right for the Australian people. What I tell you now,' Dobrogorskiy went on, 'you will not see reported anywhere. I tell you because I understand the pain you feel, and your desire to know the facts of your son's death. Truly,' he added, his voice a whisper, 'I understand only too well.' He set his eyes on the hearse once more.

'Please . . . .' the mother said with urgency.

In a stronger voice, Dobrogorskiy said, 'Geoffrey was a brave young man whose only mistake was to challenge the wrongs he saw being committed against Prime Minister Whitlam. I came here today out of respect for your son. I am not sure how much comfort this will bring you, but you should know that Geoffrey's actions very likely saved the Prime Minister from assassination. His courage in this, I am sorry to say, will never be recognised.'

Nothing more was said.

Epilogue – the following is true

Prime Minister Whitlam fought the election of 13 December 1975, believing the Australian people would maintain their rage at the dismissal of his elected government. They did not. Whitlam campaigned with the slogan *Shame, Fraser, Shame*, while the Leader of the Opposition, Malcolm Fraser, campaigned with *Turn on the Lights*. The latter was a reference to Australia's poor economy at the time. In the end, people's voting decisions were based on their wallets and Fraser won by a landslide, a result that instantly removed the uncertainty hanging over Australia's relationship with the CIA.

While Fraser enjoyed the trappings of power, Governor-General Sir John Kerr, the Queen's representative, enjoyed the wrath of the Australian people. In Whitlam's famous dismissal speech on the steps of Parliament House, he said, "Well may we say God save the Queen because *nothing* will save the Governor-General." And nothing did. The legacy of Whitlam's dismissal haunted Kerr for the rest of his life and, despite being showered with honours by the Queen, he died a broken and lonely man in 1991.

To this day, suspicion remains as to whether or not Kerr's actions were guided by the Anglo-American intelligence community, in part because of his wartime and post-war associations with that community. What has become clear, however, is that Prince Charles and Sir Martin Charteris (the Queen's Private Secretary) knew of Kerr's intention to dismiss Whitlam before the 1975 crisis. It is not known whether the Queen herself knew in advance because the letters between Kerr and the Palace have been classified as 'private' (i.e. not official Commonwealth records). At the time of writing, Kerr's letters are embargoed until at least 2027, after which the Queen retains an indefinite veto over their release.

Fraser renewed the lease for the American military spy base near Alice Springs shortly after being sworn in as Prime Minister. Commonly referred to as Pine Gap because of its location in the Pine Gap valley of the MacDonnell Ranges, the base remains one of the CIA's most important assets, capable of intercepting communications from almost anywhere, and involving extensive participation of the American National Security Agency (NSA) and the British Government Communications Headquarters (GCHQ).

On 23 August 1977, Fraser's government approved the mining and export of Australia's uranium reserves in the form of "yellowcake" (i.e. non-enriched uranium). This move effectively ended Whitlam's plans to maximise profit from those reserves by developing an enrichment plant on Australian soil. Ominously, those plans called for a collaborative project with Japan to develop a more efficient enrichment method. Had Whitlam succeeded in this endeavor, it may have ended America's domination of the industry and destroyed their control of foreign nuclear programmes. A US Congressional report on nuclear cooperation, published 1 December 2010, clearly shows that Washington took a very dim view of the discussions on uranium between Australia and Japan.

Whitlam often shied away from the question of whether or not the CIA was involved in his dismissal, though he did raise the issue in the House two years after he was sacked. On 4 May 1977, while Leader of the Opposition, he told Parliament, "There is increasing and profoundly disturbing evidence that foreign espionage and intelligence activities are being practised in Australia on a wide scale." Whitlam noted that those making the allegations "were not fanatics, crackpots or headline-seekers" but "men who have worked inside the CIA and become disenchanted with its methods". Among others, he named Victor Marchetti and Christopher Boyce.

Marchetti had helped to establish Pine Gap and is frequently reported to have said that Whitlam's threat to shut it down "caused apoplexy in the White House". More alarming still, though curiously not often reported, is his claim that "the British were probably instrumental in getting rid of Whitlam, perhaps more than the United States". If the latter is true, it is likely because Whitlam wanted all of the country's natural resources to be controlled and owned by Australians, not just uranium. With typical flair, Whitlam once said, "Foreigners do Australians the honour of employing them to dig up their own wealth, to be exported overseas." Had Whitlam succeeded in his plans it would have decimated massive investments by Britain's establishment elite, made principally through the Rio Tinto Group (formally Rio Tinto-Zinc).

Christopher Boyce was responsible for monitoring communications from Pine Gap. Disgusted by what he had heard, Boyce passed information to the Soviet Union in the hope of damaging the American intelligence community. In April 1977, he was convicted of espionage and sentenced to forty years imprisonment. At his trial, Boyce testified that the CIA had infiltrated Australian trade unions and was actively deceiving

Whitlam over activities at Pine Gap. He also testified that the CIA referred to the Governor-General as "our man Kerr". Shortly after his trial, President Jimmy Carter sent his Deputy Secretary of State, Warren Christopher, to Australia for the express purpose of promising Whitlam "the United States would never again interfere with the domestic political processes of Australia".

The Nugan-Hand Bank collapsed in 1980, shortly after Frank Nugan was discovered shot dead on the outskirts of Lithgow, New South Wales. A business card from William Colby (CIA Director, 1973–76) was found in Nugan's wallet. His partner, Michael Hand, was last seen fleeing Australia under a false identity in June 1981. The following year, the *Wall Street Journal* accused the CIA of using Nugan-Hand as a conduit for funds to assist in overthrowing Whitlam.

The whole truth of who was involved in the dismissal, and why, may never be known. It is fair to say, however, that those seeking to deny any link between Whitlam's dismissal and the USA's desire to protect its monopoly of uranium enrichment, or the CIA's interests at Pine Gap, or the longing of Britain's ruling elite to hang on to their riches, have rather a lot of evidence to sweep away. Only this much is certain: the total surveillance state, as depicted by whistle-blower Edward J Snowden, has been a long time in the making.

Stephen J Anderson

Acknowledgements

This novel is a work of fiction but is set against the background of Prime Minister Whitlam's dismissal on 11 November 1975. For readers interested in the facts on which this story is based, I recommend *A Secret Country* by John Pilger (Vintage, 1992), the biographical work *Gough Whitlam: His Time* by Jenny Hocking (The Miegunyah Press, 2012), the article *Dirty Tricks Down Under* by Phillip Frazer (Mother Jones, 1984), *The Crimes of Patriots* by Jonathan Kwitny (Norton, 1987), and *The Dismissal* by Paul Kelly and Troy Bramston (Viking, 2015).

Further evidence that foreign agencies manipulated Australian domestic affairs during Whitlam's era can be found in the Cabinet Records of 1977 from the National Archives of Australia, transcripts of the Christopher Boyce trial (*The United States of America versus Christopher John Boyce, 27 April 1977*), the account of Boyce's capture and trial in *The Falcon and the Snowman* by Robert Lindsey (Penguin Books, 1981), and Ray Martin's interview with Boyce (60 Minutes, 23 May 1982).

Evidence of Whitlam's determination to proceed with the development of uranium enrichment facilities can be found in his press statement of 12 March 1975 (# 468: Oil and Uranium Exploration). Details about Australia's proposed collaboration with Japan for uranium enrichment are reported in Wayne

Reynolds' paper *Australia's Quest to Enrich Uranium and the Whitlam Government's Loans Affair* (Australian Journal of Politics and History, 2008).

Details of the physical and organizational structure of the CIA base near Alice Springs, and its capability to undertake military and intelligence operations, were taken from *A Suitable Piece of Real Estate: American Installations in Australia* by Desmond Ball (Hale & Iremonger, 1980). Ball cites 'Merino' as the original CIA code name for the American base. Further information on the structure and day-to-day running of the base were obtained from *Inside Pine Gap: The Spy Who Came in from the Desert* by David Rosenberg (Hardie Grant Books, 2011).

I thank my big sister (that's big as in older, not big as in wider), Susan Tognela, for turning my initial ramblings into something that someone might want to read, and Dexter Petley, Tony Hayes, Tim Meese and Cherry Mosteshar for advice and constructive criticism on earlier drafts of this work.

About the author: Stephen Anderson was born and raised in Australia, and now lives in the Cotswolds of England. A cognitive neuroscientist by training, he has worked in Perth and on both sides of the Atlantic. While in Perth, an impromptu visit to a lecture by former prime minister Edward Gough Whitlam sparked an idea that eventually became the novel *Twelve Miles from Alice*. Stephen also has Mr Whitlam to thank for ending conscription to Vietnam and abolishing university tuition fees!

Stephen J Anderson
Gloucestershire, England, 15th January 2020

151

Printed in Great Britain
by Amazon

37771971R00147